*A complete list
of St. Martin's Classics
will be found at the end
of this book.*

St. Martin's Classics

NEIGHBORS UNKNOWN

"SHE FELT HER HOMELESSNESS KEENLY."

St. Martin's Classics

NEIGHBORS UNKNOWN

BY

CHARLES G. D. ROBERTS

AUTHOR OF "KINGS IN EXILE", "THE BACKWOODSMEN",
"THE HOUSE IN THE WATER", ETC.

ILLUSTRATED BY PAUL BRANSOM

TORONTO: THE MACMILLAN COMPANY OF
CANADA LIMITED, AT ST. MARTIN'S HOUSE

Copyright, Canada, 1924

BY

THE MACMILLAN COMPANY OF CANADA, LIMITED

Printed in Canada

To

PATRICIA

INTRODUCTION

CHARLES G. D. ROBERTS was born in 1860 at Douglas, New Brunswick, into an atmosphere not easily to be found in Canada to-day. The American continent had not begun to feel the surge of its own educational demands, and Canada at least was content to move easily along in the English educational tradition. This was most true, and still is, of the Maritime Provinces, and Roberts as a boy lived and moved against the background of his father's classical scholarship. That such background contributed greatly to his literary equipment cannot be denied, but many will feel that it developed standards of appreciation out of tune with Canadian life as it was, and even more as it came to be, and in the end stood between the author and the fullest realization of the world in which he lived.

Shortly after the author's birth his father, the Reverend Canon George Goodridge Roberts, M.A., LL.D., became rector of Fredericton, and it was in that lovely old New Brunswick town that the Roberts children grew up. Five of them developed outstanding literary talent, Charles, Elizabeth Roberts Macdonald, William Carman Roberts, Theodore Goodridge Roberts, and Goodridge Bliss Roberts who died when still a young man; and it is interesting to picture that group of imaginative children, playing their games of high adventure and sharing the thrills of their reading with one another. We know, too, that their father read aloud a great deal to them, and the knowledge conjures up a pleasant picture of that group before a crackling open fire listening to him reading. Probably there were interruptions while one asked a question, or another made a statement which provoked lively discussion. It was a setting calculated to develop active intellects in the children, and perhaps it might be taken as a formula for the production of young writers. Certainly the facts in the Roberts' case support such an assumption, and both in Canada and elsewhere rectories have produced a large proportion of the men of letters.

During this period of growth and for years afterward, Charles G. D. Roberts learned much of the animal and bird life of the New Brunswick woods and shores. It was a knowledge which is only gained by lovers of wild life after many nights and days spent in the open, with the eye of an artist quick to observe and sympathize in the daily tragedies and triumphs of nature. Those days and nights which form the background for Roberts' nature poetry and animal stories have made in their way as important a contribution to his literary training as the life of the rectory and his school and university courses. The latter supplied his technique, the former his material. It is no part of this introduction to consider what Roberts has written outside the field of nature.

For younger readers Charles G. D. Roberts' fame rests very surely on his stories of animal life. It is no small achievement to have produced a large body of work, the literary technique of which is acknowledged by critics to be excellent, and whose popularity surpasses that of any living writer among the high school population of at least two countries. The author's animal stories assume that wild creatures think much as we do, and that the community of the wilderness is made up of like society of rogues and saints, of robbers and good citizens. Similarly, that community is engaged in one primary pursuit, that of living. Their requirements are fewer and based on the broad necessities of life in the woods and streams: food, shelter, and a place to rear their young. Around these needs, as around our own, but infinitely more primitively, plays the incessant struggle of life and death regulated by the unchanged law of life (in the elimination of which alone we are more civilized), the survival of the fittest.

Fitness is a relative term in the wilds, as it is in our own society where the strong man is not any surer of being successful than one who is weaker but more clever. And through Charles G. D. Roberts' stories the reader finds fitness in animals to be made up of various forces which, having regard to the essential differences in the life, may be compared with the characteristics, qualities, and abilities around us. The fox frequently avoids dangers and achieves his purposes by cunning, the lynx by ferocity in attack and swiftness, the little kingbird by daring and his ability to fight in the air more dexterously in swerve, dart and dive, than any fighting aeroplane.

These are things which readers still at school, loving the camp and canoe trip, know more of perhaps than their elders. For they have seen the setting for these stories, have themselves watched a kingfisher hover, seemingly aimless over the edge of some quiet water for many minutes and then, with wings folded, drop headlong like a leaded weight, strike with a shallow splash and rise up to a nearby tree with a little twisting silver bar in its beak.

Of the tales which follow it is but faint praise to say that the style is sound. It has a magic of its own at times which makes us feel this sureness of touch. It is of a piece with the scene it depicts, being at all times filled with life and action. Through every story runs a chain of shining words; every word which describes the action of some wild creature is essentially the right one. It is not for us to say whether this is a spontaneous or studied effect. There it is, so flawless that it lifts a trifle light as gossamer into the realm of the convincing. Mood by mood we thrill, triumph and grieve with the animal folk. . . .

St. Martin's House,
    August, 1933.

CONTENTS

ILLUSTRATIONS

ON THE ROOF OF THE WORLD

"FROM TIME TO TIME THE PROWLER RAISED HIS HEAD."

On the Roof of the World

IT seemed to be the very roof of the world, all naked to the outer cold, this flat vast of solitude, dimly outspread beneath the Arctic night. A line of little hills, mere knobs and hummocks, insignificant under the bitter starlight, served to emphasize the immeasurable and shelterless flatness of the surrounding expanse. Somewhere beneath the unfeatured levels the sea ended and the land began, but over all lay the monotony of ridged ice and icy, wind-scourged snow. The wind, which for weeks without a pause had torn screaming across the nakedness, had now dropped into calm; and with the calm there seemed to come in the unspeakable cold of space.

Suddenly a sharp noise, beginning in the dimness far to the left of the Little Hills, ran snapping past them and died off abruptly in the distance to the right. It was the ice, thickened under that terrific cold, breaking in order to readjust itself to the new pressure. There was a moment of strange muttering and grinding. Then, again, the stillness.

Yet, even here on the roof of the world, which
seemed as if all the winds of eternity had swept it
bare, there was life, life that clutched and clung
savagely.   Away to the right of the Little Hills,
something moved, prowling slowly among the long
ridges of the ice.   It was a gaunt, white, slouch-
ing, startling shape, some seven or eight feet in
length, and nearly four in height, with heavy
shoulders, and a narrow, flat-browed head that
hung low and swayed menacingly from side to
side as it went.   Had the light been anything
more than the wide glimmer of stars, it would
have shown that this lonely, prowling shape of
white had a black-tipped muzzle, black edges
to the long slit of its jaws, and little, cruel eyes
with lids outlined in black.   From time to time
the prowler raised his head, sniffed with dilating
nostrils, and questioned with strained ears the
deathly silence.   It was a polar bear, an old male,
too restless and morose to content himself with
sleeping away the terrible polar winter in a snow-
blanketed hole.

From somewhere far off to seaward came across
the stillness a light sound, the breaking of thin
ice, the tinkle of splashings frozen as they fell.
The great white bear understood that sound.
He had been waiting for it.   The seals were
breaking their way up into their air-holes to

breathe — those curious holes which form here and there in the ice-fields over moving water, as if the ocean itself had need of keeping in touch with upper air for its immeasurable breathing. At a great pace, but noiselessly as a drifting wraith of snow, the bear went towards the sound. Then suddenly he dropped flat and seemed to vanish. In reality he was crawling, crawling steadily towards the place of the air-holes. But so smooth was his movement, so furtive, and so fitted to every irregularity of the icy surface, that if the eye once lost him it might strive in vain to pick him up again.

Nearer, nearer he crept, till at last, lying motionless with his lean muzzle just over the crest of the ice-ridge, he could make out the dark shapes of the seals, vague as shadows, emerging for a few moments to sprawl upon the edge of the ice. Every few seconds one would slip into the water again, while another would awkwardly scramble forth. In that phenomenal cold it was necessary for them to take heed to the air-holes, lest these should get sealed up and leave them to drown helplessly under the leagues of solid ice-field. These breathing-spells in the upper air, out here on the world's roof, were their moments of greatest peril. Close to the edge of the hole they sprawled; and always one or another kept anxious watch, scanning with mild, bright eyes the menacing solitude, wherein they seemed the only things alive.

About this time, from one of a group of tiny, snow-covered mounds huddled along the base of the Little Hills, emerged a man. He crawled forth on all fours from the tunnel of his doorway, and stood up and peered about him. His squat figure was clothed and hooded in furs. His little, twinkling eyes, after clearing themselves from the smoke and smart of the thick air within the igloo, could see further through the gloom than even the eyes of the bear. He noted the fall of the wind, the savage intensity of the cold, and his eyes brightened with hope. He had no fear of the cold, but he feared the hunger which was threatening the lonely village. During the long rage of the wind, the supply of food in his igloo had run low. He welcomed a cold which would close up most of the seals' breathing-holes, and force more numerous visitors to the few holes that they could keep open. For some moments he stood motionless, peering and listening as the bear had done. Suddenly he too caught that far-off light crashing of brittle ice. On the instant he turned and crawled hastily back into the hut.

A moment later he reappeared, carrying two weapons, besides the long knife stuck in his girdle.

One of these was an old Hudson Bay Company's musket. The other was a spear of spliced bone, with a steel head securely lashed to it. Powder and ball for the musket were much too precious to be expended, except in some emergency wherein the spear might fail. Without waiting for a repetition of the sounds, he started off at once unerringly in the direction whence they had come. He knew that air-hole; he could find it in the delusive gloom without the aid of landmark. For some way he went erect and in haste, though as soundlessly as the bear. Then, throwing himself flat, he followed exactly the bear's tactics, till, at last, peering cautiously over a jagged ice-ridge, he, too, could make out the quarry watchfully coming and going about the brink of the air-hole.

From this point onward the man's movements were so slow as to be almost imperceptible. But for his thick covering of furs, his skin tough as leather and reeking with oil, he would have been frozen in the midst of his journey. But the still excitement of the hunt was pumping the blood hotly through his veins. He was now within gunshot, but in that dim light his shooting would be uncertain. He preferred to worm his way nearer, and then trust to his more accustomed weapon, the spear, which he could drive half-way through the tough bulk of a walrus.

At last there remained between him and the seals but one low ridge and then a space of level floe. This was the critical point. If he could writhe his body over the crest and down the other side, he would be within safe spear-shot. He would spring to his feet and throw before the nimblest seal could gain the water. He lay absolutely still, summoning wits, nerves, and muscles alike to serve his will with their best. His eyes burned deep in his head, like smouldering coals.

Just at this moment a ghostly light waved broadly across the solitude. It paled, withdrew, wavered back and forth as shaken from a curtain in the heavens, then steadied ephemerally into an arch of glowing silver, which threw the light of a dozen moons. There were three seals out upon the ice at that moment, and they all lifted their eyes simultaneously to greet the illumination. The man irresistibly looked up; but in the same instant, remembering the hunger in the igloo, he cowered back again out of sight, trembling lest some of the seals might have caught a glimpse of his head above the ridge. Some dozen rods away, at the other side of the air-hole, the great white bear also raised his eyes towards that mysterious light, troubled at heart because he knew it was going to hamper his hunting.

For perhaps two minutes the seals were motionless, profiting by the sudden brightness to scrutinize the expanse of ice and snow in every direction. Then, quite satisfied that no danger was near, they resumed their sportive plungings while the instantly frozen waters crackled crisply about them. For all their vigilance, they had failed to detect, on the one side, a narrow, black-tipped muzzle lying flat in a cleft of the ice-ridge, or, on the other side, a bunch of grayish fur, nearly the color of the grayish-mottled ice, which covered the head of the man from the igloo beside the Little Hills.

And now, while neither the man nor the bear, each utterly unconscious of the other, dared to stir, in a flash the still silver radiance of the aurora broke up and flamed into a riot of dancing color. Parallel rays like the pipes of a Titanic organ, reaching almost from the horizon to the zenith, hurtled madly from side to side, now elongating, now shortening abruptly, now seeming to clash against one another, but always in an ordered madness of right lines. Unearthly green, palpitating into rose, and thinnest sapphire, and flame-color, and ineffably tender violet, the dance of these cohorts of the magnetic rays went on, across the stupendous arc of sky, till the man, afraid of freezing in his unnatural stillness, shrank back down the ridge, and began twisting his body, noiselessly but violently, to set his blood in motion; and the bear, trusting to the confusion of shifting lights, slipped himself over the ridge and into a convenient crevice. Under the full but bewildering glare of that celestial illumination, he had gained a good ten feet upon his human rival. The man's eyes reappeared just then at the crest of his ridge. Their piercing glance lingered, as if with suspicion, upon the crevice wherein the bear had flattened himself. Was there something unduly solid in that purple shadow in the crevice? No, a trick of the witch lights, surely. The piercing eyes returned to their eager watching of the seals.

Precious as was his ammunition, and indifferent as was his shooting with the old, big bore, Hudson Bay musket, the man was beginning to think he would have to stake his chances on the gun. But, suddenly, as if at a handsweep of the Infinite, the great lights vanished.

For a few seconds, by the violence of the contrast, it seemed as if thick darkness had fallen upon the world.

In those few seconds, noiseless and swift as a panther, the man had run over the ridge to within a dozen paces of the seals, and paused with spear uplifted, waiting till his eyes should once more be able to see in the starlight glimmer. As he stood thus waiting, every sense, nerve, and muscle on the last strain of expectancy and readiness, he heard, or seemed to feel as much as to hear, the rush of some great bulk through the gloom. Then came a scramble, a heavy splash, a second splash, a terrible scuffling noise, and a hoarse, barking scream. The man remembered that before the light went out there had been three seals on the ice. Two he had heard escape. What had befallen the third? Fiercely, like a beast being robbed of its prey, he sprang forward a couple of paces. Then he stopped, for he could not yet see clearly enough to distinguish what was before him. His blood pounded through his veins. The cold of Eternity was flowing in upon him, here on the naked roof of the world, but he had no feeling or fear of it. All he felt was the presence of his foe, there before him, close before him, in the dark.

Then, once more, the light flooded back, — the wide-flung silver radiance, — as suddenly and mysteriously as it had vanished.

Close beside the air-hole, half crouching upon the body of the slain seal, with one great paw uplifted, and bloody jaws open in defiance, stood the bear, glaring at the man.

Without an instant's hesitation the man hurled

his spear. It flew true. But in that same second the bear lifted his paw to ward off the blow. He was not quite quick enough, but almost. The blade struck, but not where it was aimed. It bit deep, but not to the life. With a growl of rage, the bear tore it loose and charged upon the man.

The antagonists were not more than twenty paces apart, and now a glory of colored lights, green, red, and golden, went dancing madly over them, with a whispering, rustling sound as of stiff silk crumpled in vast folds. The man's eyes were keen and steady. In a flash both hands were out of his great fur mittens, which were tied by thongs to his sleeves. The heavy musket leaped to his shoulder, and his eye ran coolly along the barrel. There was a thunderous roar as of a little cannon. A dense cloud of smoke sprang into the air just before the muzzle of the gun.

Through the smoke a towering shape, with wide jaws and battering paws, hurled itself. The man leaped to one side, but not quite far enough. One great paw, striking blindly, smote him down; and, as he fell, the huge bulk fell half upon him, only to roll over the next instant and lie huddled and motionless upon the ice.

The man picked himself up, shook himself; and a look of half-dazed triumph went across his swarthy face as he pulled on his mittens. Then he smiled broadly, patted approvingly the old Hudson Bay musket, turned on his heels, and sent a long, summoning cry across the ice towards the igloos at the foot of the Little Hills.

BLACK SWAMP

Black Swamp

THE brook, which had rattled down so gayly, with many a laughing rapid and clattering white cascade, from the sunlit granite terraces of Lost Mountain, fell silent and hung back as it drew near the swamp. Wheeling in slow, deep, purple-dark eddies, it loitered for some hundred yards or so between dim overhanging ranks of alder, then sank reluctantly beneath an arch of mossed cedar-roots, and was lost in the heavy gloom.

Within the swamp the huge and ancient trunks of cedar and tamarack crowded in a sort of desperate confusion. Of great girth at the base, some towered straight up, seeking to get their tops out into the sunlight, under those sparse patches of far-off, indifferent sky. Others slanted ponderously, and laid upon their neighbors the responsibility of supporting their burden of massive branches. Yet others, undermined in youth by some treachery of the slough, lay prone above the water-holes for a portion of their length, and then turned skyward, ineffectually, as if too late awakened from their sluggish dreams. The roots of the trees were half uncovered — immense, coiled, uncouth, dull-colored shapes, like monsters struggling up from the teeming primeval slime.

In truth, there was a suggestion of something monstrous in all that the eye could see in Black Swamp. The heavy, indeterminate masses of dark mud, or patches of black water, lying deep between and under the contortions of the roots; the thick, gray rags of dead cedar-bark; the rotting stumps, some uprooted and half engulfed in the inert morass; the overpowering windless shadow, which lay thick as if no sound had ever jarred it; above all, the gigantic tangle of trunks and roots, stagnantly motionless, with the strained stillness that is not of peace, but of a nightmare. From a branch of one of the sullen trunks hung a globe of lightest-gray papery substance, with a round hole in the bottom of it. In and out of this hole moved two venomous streams of black-and-white hornets.

Suddenly it seemed as if the spirit of the monstrous solitude had taken substance, and was moving among the inert shapes of root and trunk. A massive fur-clad beast, dull black in color, with high, humped haunches and heavy, shapeless limbs, its hind feet grotesquely semi-human in outline, its head swinging low on a long, clumsy neck, came picking its way with a loose-jointed gait over the jumble of roots. With little, twinkling, deep-set eyes it peered beneath each root, investigated each crevice in the ancient bark, looking for grubs and beetles, which its great paws captured with amazing though awkward-looking dexterity. For so huge a beast as the great black bear, which could pull down an ox, to busy himself in the hunting of grubs and beetles, seemed one of the whimsicalities of Nature, who pursues her ends indifferently through mammoth or microbe.

Near the tree of the hornets the bear found a half-rotten stump. Sniffing at it with instructed nose, he decided that it held grubs. Clutching at it with his long, hooked claws, he tore away one side of it, revealing a mellow-brown, crumbly interior channelled by wood-grubs in every direction. Those which were in view on the erect portion of the stump he first picked out delicately and devoured with satisfaction. Then he turned his attention to the big slab which he had ripped away, and which lay on a hummock of firm ground at his feet.

But the bear was not the only connoisseur of grubs in Black Swamp. Some dozen inches before his nose a particularly fat maggot was squirming in the shallow remnant of its chamber, dismayed at its sudden exposure to the air. The bear was just on the point of picking it up,

when it was pounced upon by one of the great
black-and-white hornets, as a hawk might pounce
on a rabbit. Pricked with the tip of the hornet's
sting, the fat grub lashed itself out in one convulsive squirm, and then lay still. Straddling
over it, the hornet rolled it together cleverly,
then, plunging her mandibles into its soft body,
proceeded to drain its juices.

For some moments the bear had watched this
performance with curious interest, his little eyes
twinkling wickedly. Now he had had enough
of the show. Stretching out one mighty paw,
he laid it down deliberately on the hornet and her
prey. For a moment he left it there, as if his
act had been one of considered punishment.
Then, withdrawing the paw, he eyed the flattened
insect, and proceeded to swallow her and her
victim together.

But the hornet was not quite dead, for the
rotten wood was soft and full of unevenness;
and this insect, with its burnished black body
barred with creamy white, was no mere peppery
little " yellow-jacket " wasp, but the great hornet
of the woods, whose sting can pierce the hide of
the moose. No sooner had the bear picked up
the dangerous morsel than he spat it out again with
a *woof* of surprise, and ground it into nothingness
with an angry sweep of his paw. Then he fell to

shaking his head, clawing awkwardly at his mouth, and whining a fretful protest at the sting. Lumbering down to a swamp-hole close by, he plunged his muzzle again and again into the chill black mud.   After a brief period of this treatment, he returned to the stump and went on with his banquet of grubs, stopping every now and then to shake his head and grumble deep in his throat. When another big hornet, catching sight of the feast, pounced upon a grub, he smashed her and ground her up instantly, without caring how many tasty morsels were annihilated in the process.

When the stump had been quite torn to pieces, and every maggot extracted from it, the bear moved on to the tree of the hornets. He did not notice the nest, for he did not take the trouble to look up.   If he had done so, being in a rage against the venomous tribe, he might, perhaps, have had the rashness to climb the tree and declare a doubtful war.   As it was, he noted only that between two great roots, which sprang out like buttresses from the base of the trunk, there was a space of dry earth, covered with the minute elastic needles of the tamarack.   Here he threw himself down with a grunt, and fell to rubbing his face with his thick forepaws.

But he was restless, the old bear — either be·

cause the grubs had not satisfied his hunger, or because the sting of the hornet still rankled in his jaw. Almost immediately he got up upon his haunches, and stared all about, sniffing, with his nose in the air. The monstrous confusion of roots and trunks, monotonously repeating itself as far as he could see through the shadow, appeared to offer him nothing worth his attention. But presently he lurched forward, as if he had made up his mind what to do. Shambling grotesquely, but picking his way above the slime as delicately as a cat, he kept on for perhaps a hundred yards. Perhaps his nostrils had caught, across the stagnant air, the tang of running water. It was running water that he came to, for the brook, though often foiled, often diverted, often turned back upon itself, and almost lost, had succeeded in saving for itself a clean channel through the water-holes and chaos of the swamp.

Just at this point the brook ran through a dark but living pool, brown but transparent, with here and there a gleam of elusive light, as in the eyes of some dark-eyed women. To this pool, and others like it strung here and there through the swamp, had gathered many fish, — trout, suckers, and chub, — fleeing the too direct rays of the high midsummer sun.

Lumbering down the sticky bank, the bear

squatted himself on his haunches close to the edge of the water, and stared at it fixedly. After a time his eyes began to discern the fish which thronged in its deep centre. Having assured himself that the fish were there, he lay down on his stomach, in a hunched, shapeless position, with his face close to the water and one paw uplifted. It looked like a difficult position to hold, but the bear held it, motionless as one of the great roots, and quite as inert-looking, till by and by some of the fish, which had been frightened away by his coming, swam slowly back to the weedy edges to feed. These fish were suckers, weed-eaters, thick-bodied and sluggish in movement, very different from the swift, ravening trout. A spark flashed into the deep of the bear's eyes as he saw them coming, but not so much as the edge of a nostril quivered. A big sucker with a snout that overhung, and opened and shut greedily, came nosing the mud close up under his face. With a lightning scoop the waiting paw descended, and the fish, amid a noisy splashing, was hurled out upon the bank, half stunned. Before it could recover itself enough to flop, the bear was upon it. Picking it up between his jaws, he carried it lazily back to that dry couch he had found beneath the tree of the hornets, there to be eaten at his leisure.

While the bear, ponderous and sullen, was mumbling over his meal in that uncouth solitude, there came, moving briskly down the brook's margin, a gay little figure that seemed an embodied protest against all the dark and enormous formlessness of the swamp. It was as if the world of sunlight, and swift motion, and bright vitality, and completed form, had sent in its herald to challenge the inertness of the gloom.

The tripping little figure was about the size of a fox, and with the long, pointed, inquisitive muzzle of a fox. Its abundant fur was of a cloudy, irregular yellowish-gray, darkening at the tips, and shading to almost black along the back. Its tail was long, light, and vividly barred with black. Its dainty, fine-clawed, hand-like feet were bright black. But the most striking thing about it was its face, which was very light gray, with a large black patch around each eye like an exaggerated pair of spectacles. The eyes themselves were extraordinarily large, dark, and lustrous, and glowed with a startling, almost impish intelligence.

The raccoon was not given, as a rule, to daytime prowlings, his preference being for moonlight rather than sunlight. Nor, usually, was he given to haunting the sinister recesses of Black Swamp. But he was a wanderer, and capricious as all vagabonds ; and he had somehow discovered that there were crawfish in the brook where it flowed through the swamp. He was an ardent fisherman, deft and unerring with his hand-like claws. But to-day his fishing was unsuccessful, for never a crawfish was so considerate as to come his way. He saw the suckers and trout gathered at the mid-deeps of the pools, but he was too impatient, or not really hungry enough, to wait for them to come near shore. While he was watching beside the big pool wherein the bear had recently fished with such success, a wood-mouse unwarily came out of its hole, just at his feet, and was captured before it had time to see its peril. This prize contented the raccoon. Having killed his victim instantly with a cheerful nip behind the ears, he sat by the pool's edge and proceeded to souse the morsel vigorously up and down in the water before eating it. Not until it was washed almost to a rag did he seem to think it clean enough to eat, and then, after all his trouble, he nibbled hardly the half of it, flinging the remnant into the water with the air of a wasteful child who has never known what it feels like to go hungry.

From the edge of the brook the raccoon ran up the bank. After a pause he turned aimlessly into the still turmoil of the trunks and roots. Every fallen trunk, every long tentacle of a root that he came to, he would mount it and run along it to the end in whatever direction it led. As the luck of the wild would have it, this erratic progress brought him presently to one of the great buttressing roots of the tree of the hornets. He mounted it, of course, followed it nearly to the base of the trunk, and stopped abruptly at the sight of the bear.

The bear, who had but recently finished his meal of fish, was lying half asleep on the dry tamarack needles between the roots. He had well eaten, but the sting in his mouth still fretted him, and his mood was ugly. His great head was moving sullenly, ponderously, from side to side. Ominous and dark and ill-shapen, he looked strangely like a portion of the swamp come alive. The raccoon scrutinized him with eyes of bright, mischievous disdain. The bear, looking up, caught sight of him, and aimed a treacherous blow at him with his tremendous, armed forepaw. Light as a feather, the raccoon avoided him. It was as if the very wind of the blow had swept him from the place of danger. The bear grunted at his failure, and fell to licking his paw. The raccoon, who had slipped around the tree, mounted another root, and gazed at his rude assailant impishly. Then, glancing upwards, his liquid eyes detected the pendent gray globe of the hornets' nest, pale in the gloom.

The raccoon knew that inside every hornets' nest or wasps' nest at this time of the year was a mass of peculiarly succulent larvæ and immature insects. If this gray globe had been a wasps' nest, he might, perhaps, have attacked it at once, his long hair, thick skin, and skill in protecting his eyes, enabling him to brave, without too great cost, the stings of the ordinary "yellow-jacket." But he noted well the formidable insects which hummed about this nest; he knew the powers of the black-and-white hornet. Having stared at the nest for several minutes, he seemed to come to some decision. Thereupon he tripped off delicately over the tree-roots to the brook, to resume his hunt for crawfish.

It was by this time getting far along in the afternoon. As the gloom deepened at the approach of twilight, the bear went to sleep. The darkness fell thicker and thicker, till his breathing bulk could no longer be distinguished from the trunk beside it. Then, from narrow openings in the far-off tree-tops, fell here and there a ray of white moonlight, glassy clear, but delusive. Under the touch of these scant rays, every shrouded mystery of the swamp took on a sort of malignant life.

About this time the raccoon came back. In that phantom illumination, more treacherous than the dark, his wide eyes, nearly all pupil, saw as clearly as in the daylight. They gleamed elvishly as they took note of the sleeping bear. Then they glanced upward toward the hornets' nest, where it hung just crossed by one chill white pencil of a moon ray. Softly their owner ran up the tree, his delicate claws almost inaudible as they clutched the roughness of the bark.

At the base of the slim branch — hardly more than a twig, but alive and tough — which held the nest of the hornets, the raccoon stopped. He wanted the contents of that nest. But he did not want to test the prowess of its guardians, which were now, as he well knew, all within, too heavy with sleep to fly, but as competent as ever to sting. After some moments of deliberation, he bit the twig through and let the nest fall. Then he scrambled hastily down the tree, as if eager to see what would happen.

His purpose, perhaps, in dropping the nest was simply a wanton impulse to destroy what he desired but could not have. Perhaps he thought the nest would roll into a shallow pool at the other side of the tree, and so drown its occupants, after which he might rifle it at his own convenience. Or, possibly, he calculated that

that would happen which presently did. The
nest fell, not into the water, but between the
upcurled forepaws, and very close to the nose, of
the slumbering bear.

The bear, awakened and startled by its light
fall, growled and bit angrily at the intruding nest.
At the same time, with an instinctive clutch, he
ripped it open, not realizing just what it was.
The next instant he knew. With a *woof* of rage,
he tried to crush it and all its envenomed populace
within it. But he was too late. The great
hornets were already swarming over him, crawling, burrowing deep into the fur about his face
and neck and belly. Furiously they plunged
and replunged their long, flame-like stings. His
eyes and muzzle crawled with the fiery torment.
Clawing, striking, snapping, grunting, whimpering, he rolled over and over in desperate effort to
rid himself of the all-pervasive attack. But the
foes he crushed had already left behind their poison
in his veins. For a few moments his monstrous
contortions went on, while in a glassy patch of
white light, on the trunk above, clung the raccoon,
gazing down upon him with liquid, elvish eyes.
At length, quite beside himself with the torment, he
reared upon his hind-quarters, battling in the air.
Then he lunged forward, and went scrambling
headlong over the slippery black jumble of roots.

The great beast's first impulse, one may guess, was simply that of flight, of mad effort to escape from foes whom he could not cope with. Having no heed of his direction, the blind guidance of trunk and root led him around in a rough circle, till he came almost back to the tree of his fate. Between him and the tree, however, lay a spacious patch of morass, fairly firm on the surface, but underneath, a slough of viscous mud. His eyes almost closed by the stings, the bear plunged straight forward into this morass. His first instinct was to struggle frantically back, but as he fell, his nose had dipped into the mud. The chill of it was like a balm to his tortured nostrils and lips. This, indeed, was what he wanted. He wallowed straight ahead, plunging his face deep into the icy slime. The drench of it soothed the scorching of his stung belly. The anguish of his eyelids was assuaged. Again and again, buried now to his shoulders, he thrust his face into the ooze. Then, with the salving of his torment, his senses seemed to return. He tried to wallow back to firm ground.

The swamp, as we have seen, was in all things monstrous. It was monstrous now to its offspring and victim, in warning him too late. The patch of morass was of great depth, and the bear was sucked under so swiftly that, even as he turned to escape, he sank to the neck. His huge forepaws beat and clawed at the stiffer surface, breaking it down into the liquid ooze beneath. Presently they also were engulfed. Only his head remained above the mud. His gaping muzzle, strained straight upward, emitted hideous gasps and groans. A beam of moonlight lay across the scene, still and malignant, and the raccoon watched from the tree with an untriumphant curiosity. When at last that terrible and despairing head had vanished, and nothing remained but a long convulsion of the mud, the raccoon came daintily down from his post of observation, and examined the remains of the hornets' nest. It was crushed and pounded quite too flat to be of any further interest to him, so, after a disdainful wrinkling of his fine black nose, he tripped away to seek again the world to which he belonged — the world of free airs, and dancing leaves, and clamoring waters, and bright, swift, various life, and yellow moonlight over the fields of corn.

THE ISLE OF BIRDS

"She saw the Dark Robber descending upon Her."

The Isle of Birds

FAR out of the track of ships, in the most desolate stretch of the North Atlantic, walled round with ceaseless thunder of the surf and wailed about continually by innumerable sea-birds, the islet thrust up its bleak rocks beneath a pale, unfriendly sky.

It was almost all rock, this little island — gray pinnacles of rock, ledges upon ledges of rock, and one high, sunrise-facing cliff of rock, seamed with transverse crevices and shelves. Only on the gentler southward slope was the rock-frame of the island a little hidden. Here had gathered a few acres of mean, sandy soil, dotted sparsely with tufts of harsh grass which struggled into greenness at the bidding of a bitter and fog-blighted June.

But this remote, sterile isle, shunned even by the whalers because of the treachery of its environing reefs and tides, was by no means lifeless. Indeed, it was thronged, packed, clamorous, screaming with life. It was a very paradise of the nesting sea-birds. Every meagre foot of it, rock and sand, was preempted and occupied by the myriad battalions of puffin, skua, auk, and saddle-back. The incessant clamor of their voices, harsh and shrill, overrode even the trampling of the surf.

Within the crowded little domain each tribe had its territory. The puffins — or "sea-parrots," as some of the sailor folk call them, because of their huge hooked beaks — occupied the sandy slope, where they had their nests in deep burrows for protection against the robber skuas and saddle-backs. The auks had a corner of the cliff-face, where along every ledge they sat straight up in prim, close array like so many dwarf penguins, each couple occupied with its precious solitary egg. The rest of the cliff-face was monopolized by the screaming hosts of the saddle-backs, those great, marauding, black-backed gulls, whose yelps and wild *ka-ka-ka-kaings* made most of the deafening tumult in which the rocks were wrapt. As for the skuas, or "men-o'-war," less numerous than the other inhabitants of the island, they occupied the lower ledges and the rock-crevices around the base of the puffins' field. These were the situations which they preferred. If they had preferred the territory of the puffins or the auks, or even of the big bullying saddle-backs which were nearly twice their size, they would have taken it. But they neither desired nor knew how to dig burrows like the droll little puffins; and they valued their precious eggs too highly to want to risk them on the narrow, exposed shelves of the cliff-face, where there was no room to make a proper nest. They took the places they wanted, but as these were not the places which the other tribes wanted, there was no one to feel aggrieved. Saddle-back, auk, and puffin — each tribe thought it had the pick of the island territory, and felt altogether satisfied with itself.

Now, the weakest of these tribes was the tribe of the puffins. But one great strength they had, which fully made up for their deficiency in size and power. They knew how to burrow deep holes for their nests, wherein their eggs and nestlings were safe from the skuas and the saddle-backs. Every available inch of soil on the island was tunnelled with these burrows, like a rabbit-warren. At the bottom of each burrow was either one big, solitary egg, or a strange-looking youngster with enormous head and beak and an insatiable appetite for fish. At this season, late June, most of the puffins had hatched out their eggs. At the doorway of almost every burrow, therefore, was to be seen one of the parents on guard, while the other was away fishing to supply the insatiable demands of the chick. In dense ranks, sitting erect like auks or penguins, the seriously grotesque little birds sentinelled their homes, maintaining a businesslike quiet in strange contrast to the ear-splitting volubility of their neighbors.

At the extreme left of the territory of the puffins, where the rocks broke abruptly, a tiny cleft-full of earth made room for just one nest. The pair of puffins who had their burrow here were comparatively isolated, being some eight or ten feet apart from the crowded ranks of their kin. Their one big egg had been safely hatched. The ridiculous chick, all gaping beak and naked belly, the one object of their passionate solicitude, was thriving and hungry according to the finest traditions of infant puffinhood. The father, at this moment, was on guard at the mouth of the burrow, sitting solemnly erect on his webbed feet, the backs of his legs, and his stiff, short tail; while the mother was away fishing beyond the white turmoil of the surf.

Surely the most curious figure of all the sea-birds was his. For the body, it was not so far out of the ordinary,—about the size of a big and sturdy cockatoo,—white below and blackish-brown above, sides of the face white, and a dingy white collar on the neck; the webbed feet of a duck; the stiff, short tail of a penguin; very short, strong wings; and a round head. But the beak was like a gaudy caricature. Curved from base to tip like a parrot's, it was as long and high as the head which it seemed to overweigh, and adorned apparently aimlessly with exaggerated horny ridges. Over each eye was a little wart-like horn, and at each corner of the beak, where it joined the skin of the face, a vivid red, wrinkled excrescence, in shape a sort of rosette, of skinny flesh. Serviceable, to be sure, this beak was obviously, whether for burrowing, fighting, or catching fish; but it could be imagined as performing all these offices equally well without its monstrous eccentricities of adornment.

Everywhere in front of the cliff-face, over the ledges, above the white shuddering of the surf, and far out over the smooth leaden-gray rollers, the air was full of whirling and beating wings. These were the wings of the giant gulls and the skuas. The puffins did no more flying than was necessary — swift and straight from their nests out to the fishing-grounds, and back with their prey to the nests. Above their little domain, therefore, the honeycombed south-sloping field, there were no soaring or whirling wings, save for three or four pirate skuas, on the watch for a chance of robbery.

It was these marauders that the waiting puffin by his nest door, on the outskirts of the colony, had most dread of. He was a wise old bird, of several seasons' experience and many a successful battle; and he knew that the light-darting skua, though not much more than half the size of that bully of the cliffs, the saddle-back, was much more dangerous than the latter because so much more courageous. An impatient croak from the hungry nestling in the burrow made him poke his big beak inside and utter a low, chuckling admonition. When he withdrew his head and looked up, he fluttered the feathers on his neck and opened his beak angrily. A large skua, of a rusty, mottled black all over, with long tail and long, hawk-like wings, was circling above him, staring down at him with savage eyes.

Just a moment or two before this the hen puffin, fishing out at sea, had marked a plump herring about a foot below the surface of a transparent, glassy roller. Diving into the water with a violent splash, she had pursued the fish in his own element, swimming at an altogether miraculous speed. To gain this speed she used not only her strong, webbed feet, but also her short, sturdy wings. Darting through the water in this fashion, just below the surface, she was an amazing figure, some fantastic link, as it were, between bird and fish. The herring was overtaken, and clutched securely in the vice of the great parrot beak. Then, with much desperate flapping and splashing, she burst forth and rose into the air, heading homeward, straight as a bullet, with her prize.

Flying close to the surface of the sea, she passed through the high-flung spray of the surf. At this moment some premonition of her coming drew her mate's eyes, and he caught sight of her, just mounting above the ledges. Following his look, the skua, whirling above his head, caught sight of her also, and marked the prey she carried in her beak. With one magnificent effortless thrust of his long pinions, he swooped to intercept her.

The puffin, her great beak and the prize it clutched looking much too big for her swiftly beating wings to upbear, was coming up over the ledges at a humming pace, when she saw the dark robber descending upon her. She swerved, and so escaped the full force of the blow; but she felt herself enveloped in a whirlwind of wings and beaten down almost to the ground. At the same time a long, straight, powerful beak, with the tip hooked like a vulture's, snapped loudly at the side of her head, grasping at the fish she carried. Bewildered and terrified as she was, she was at the same time full of fighting obstinacy. Hanging doggedly to her prize, she recovered her wing balance, and rocketed on toward her burrow.

Her mate, meanwhile, had seen the attack. One grotesque little bob of indecision, then he had launched himself down the slope to her succor. He was not in time to interfere in the first encounter, but as he came slanting down like a well-aimed missile, the robber was just about to swoop again. The indignant puffin volleyed into him from the rear, turning him almost end over end. For an instant his wings flopped frantically, and he almost came down upon the rocks. By the time he had recovered himself his assailant had struck the water and was swimming comfortably on a great gray swell beyond the surf; while the female, with the herring gripped still in her absurd beak, was just diving triumphantly into her burrow to feed the ravenous and complaining chick.

The skua was disgusted. Had he been what he in some ways so much resembled, namely, a goshawk or falcon, with a hawk's deadly talons, the encounter would have had a very different result. But his handsome black feet were armed with nothing more formidable than webs for swimming. His only weapons were his hook-tipped beak and his long, powerful, buffeting wings. Backed, however, by his pluck and his audacity, which were worthy of a better occupation, these weapons were usually sufficient, and he was not used to being balked as these two serious little householders had balked him. With a vicious yelp, he went swooping low along the sentinel ranks of the puffins, followed by a snapping of indignant beaks which crackled along the lines as he went — a curious, dry sound, audible through the deep roar of the surf and the high-pitched clamor of bird-cries. Here and there a buffet of his wing, as it dipped suddenly, would knock over one of the grotesque but dauntless doorkeepers, who would pick himself up, ruffle his feathers, and waddle back to his post with outraged solemnity.

But revenge for his recent discomfiture was not the only or the chief reason for this raid of the pirate skua over the domain of the citizen puffins. What he wanted above all was food — whether fish, or eggs, or nestlings, it was all the same to him. A fairly competent fisherman himself — though not, of course, in the same class with the puffins, because of their power of swimming under water — he nevertheless preferred to make others do his fishing for him, and to take toll of their honest gains by force. A hardy and fearless highwayman, there was satisfaction for him in the robbery itself. As he flew thus close, and with the air of set purpose, above the puffin burrows, a few desultory saddle-backs who were circling just above dipped lower to see what was going to happen. In case of a scrimmage of any sort, there was always the possibility of a chance to snatch something.

As the skua skimmed along, just ahead of him came a puffin, volleying upward from the sea with a particularly fine fish in his beak. The lucky fisherman shot straight to his hole. But, by the finest hairbreadth, the robber got there before him. There was a wild mix-up of wings. The puffin was knocked clean over on his back, losing the fish, which fell just before the next burrow. Like a flash the proprietor of that next burrow bobbed his head forward and snatched at the unexpected windfall. He caught it by the tail, and turned to plunge into the burrow with it. But in that same instant the long beak of the skua caught it by the head. For a second or so the two tugged savagely at the prize, with a vast flapping and squawking. Then the outraged owner, recovering himself, floundered up, fixed his beak in the exposed belly of the fish, and began to pull and jerk like an angry terrier.

Feathers and sand flew into the air as the triangular tug-of-war went on. But frantic as was the turmoil of scuffling and flapping, the near-by ranks of puffins paid no attention to it whatever, except to turn their great beaks, all at the same angle, and stare solemnly, like so many fantastic maskers. The gulls overhead, however, gathered down with excited cries, seeking a chance to take part in the scuffle.

But before they could get their greedy beaks into it, it had come to an end. The fish was torn apart. The puffin who had grabbed the tail fell backwards with it, ruffled but triumphant, into his burrow; the original owner was left with just so much as his beak could hold — fortunately no mean mouthful; while the too-successful marauder, bearing by far the largest share of the prize, beat vigorously aloft through the screaming gulls, who would have tried to rob him had they dared. Rising strongly above them, he headed for the flat ledge, a little inland, where he and his dusky mate had made their nest.

Meanwhile, on the neighboring cliff-face, had just occurred one of those incidents which were forever stirring up excitement among the colonies of the auks and the saddle-backs. It began in the usual way. Each pair of auks, it must be remembered, has but one egg, which is laid, with no pretence of a nest, on the bare narrow ledge. As these eggs lie side by side along the rock, just far enough apart for the parents to brood them, and as they all look amazingly alike, sometimes the owners themselves get mixed up as to the identity of their speckled property. In this instance, two mothers, on a crowded shelf some

forty feet above the sea, claimed the same egg,
and both insisted on brooding it at the same
time.   With curious, strident grumblings, deep
in their throats, they struggled over it.   Their
mates, chancing both to return from their fishing
at this moment, joined vigorously in the discussion.   The egg was promptly rolled off the ledge
and smashed on the rocks below.   But in the excitement its absence was not noticed.   Meanwhile
the combatants were making things most uncom-
fortable for their nearest neighbors, so these
presently were dragged into the fight.   The unfortunate eggs began dropping over the ledge.
Instantly the great saddle-backs, from the noisy
colony higher up the cliff, swept down to gather
in the juicy harvest.   They loved eggs, whether
fresh or half brooded.   Screaming joyously, they
thronged the air just below the scene of the quarrel, which still went on with zest.   Some of the
tumbling eggs were stabbed cleverly and sucked
in mid-air as they fell, while others were devoured
or sucked up, according to the stage of development of their contents, on the rocks below.   So
long did the foolish auks continue their quarrel,
so unusual was the rain of eggs, so wild was the
screaming of the delighted banqueters below the
ledge, that presently a number of the brooding
saddle-backs — those who should have stayed by

their charges to guard them, whatever their con-
sorts might be doing — were seduced from their
too tame responsibilities. Standing up in their
dizzy nests, — most of which held either two or
three muddy-colored eggs, scrawled with mark-
ings of dull maroon, — they stretched their fierce
yellow beaks over the brink and peered down with
predacious eyes. For many of them the temptation was not to be resisted. With hoarse cries
they launched themselves downward, and joined
deliriously in the scramble.

About level with the crest of the cliff, some
half dozen of the dusky skuas were sailing
leisurely. They saw their chance. There was
nothing in the world more to their taste than
eggs — and particularly the big, rich eggs of the
great saddle-back gulls. Down they swooped
upon the unguarded nests; and in a moment,
plunging their long beaks through the shells,
they were feasting greedily. All around them
sat the other gulls, by the hundred — faithful ones
who had resisted temptation and stuck to their
nests. These screamed angrily, but made no attempt to interfere. "Let each look out for his
own" was frankly their policy. Before any of
the delinquent brooders came back, the skuas had
cleared out every unguarded nest, and sailed off
with derisive cries.

And so it came about that an unwonted number of saddle-backs, freed from domestic ties until they should be ready to lay new clutches of eggs, but very savage and vindictive for all their release, now came flapping inland over the island on the lookout for any possible chance to avenge themselves.

At this moment the great skua who had robbed the puffin of its fish came in sight of his nest. At his approach the female, who had grown impatient, arose from her handsome, greenish-brown, mottled eggs, sprang into the air, and sailed off toward the sea. For just about ten or a dozen seconds the precious eggs were left exposed, while the male swept down to them on a long, swift glide. But in those brief seconds fate struck. With an exultant yelp a huge saddle-back dropped out of the sky, directly upon the nest, and plunged his beak into one of the eggs. The egg was not far from hatching. He dragged forth the naked chick and swallowed it ravenously. Before he could turn to another egg, the skua had fallen upon him, hurling him clear of the nest, and tearing at him with desperate beak.

Now, the great gull, fully two feet and a half in length from the tip of his punishing yellow beak to the tip of his tail, was not far from twice the size of his fearless and furious assailant. Moreover, having just had his own nest destroyed, he was in a fighting mood. Ordinarily, being a thorough bully, he would have cowered and fled before the skua's swift rage, but now he turned and struck back savagely. More nimble than he, the skua evaded the blow, and caught him by the neck. And promptly the two became entangled into a flapping, tearing jumble of beaks and feathers.

It was close beside the nest that the struggle went on ; but meanwhile the two remaining eggs were lying uncovered to the eyes of prowlers. They did not lie there long. Two more big saddle-backs straightway pounced upon them, crushing them flat in the scuffle. Engrossed though he was, the skua saw them. He was only a shameless robber, but his mettle was of a temper of the finest, and he knew not fear. Tearing himself free from his heavy foe, he pounced frantically upon these new assailants of his home. Startled, they hesitated whether to fight or flee. Then, seeing the odds so far in their favor, they turned to fight. The first saddle-back joining them, they presently succeeded in pulling the skua down. Then against their great weight and overpowering wings, his courage availed him little. Smothered, beaten, trodden upon, he disappeared from sight beneath the yelping turmoil. The odds had been too great for him. In half a minute the battle was over and his dark body, with the throat completely torn out, lay unresisting beneath the broad, pink, heavy-webbed feet of his conquerors.

Suddenly, as if at a signal, all three saddlebacks lifted their heads and stared about them. They marked their victim's mate winging upward toward them from the sea, swiftly, as if a prescience of evil had summoned her. They saw two other skuas sailing down from the cliff-top, as if to demand their business in skua territory. They had no stomach to face that demand; they had no heart for a fight on anything approaching fair terms. Flapping heavily into the air, they flew off in haste to lose themselves in the myriads of their screaming fellows. The female skua, returning, hovered low; but she did not alight. In silence, her head thrust downwards, she circled and circled endlessly on dark wings above the scattered ruins of her nest, the bedraggled and tattered body of her slain mate. And the stiff ranks of the puffins, like fantastic toy birds carved in wood and painted, stared down upon her solemnly from the slopes near by.

THE ANTLERS OF THE
CARIBOU

"The Fight hung exactly in the Balance."

The Antlers of the Caribou

> When the frost is on the barrens,
> And the popple-leaves are thinned,
> And the caribou are drifting
> Down the wind, ——

SO writes one who knows all about how autumn comes to the Tobique barrens, and who claims to know as much as most men about the caribou. But the caribou do not always drift, by any means. They are rather an incalculable folk, these caribou, — and even in their name one notes their inclination to be contrary; for the herds which frequent the high, watery barrens of northern New Brunswick are not, as one might suppose, the "caribou of the barren grounds," but the larger and warier "woodland caribou." The faithful observer of the manners and customs of this tribe may spend much time one year in learning what he will be constrained to unlearn with humility the next.

The lonely lake, smooth as a mirror between its flat, desolate shores, spread pink, amber, and gold toward the cloudless pink and orange sky, where the sun had just sunk below the wooded

53

horizon. All the way up the lake, on one side, the shore was an unbroken stretch of treeless barren. On the other side the low, dark, serried ranks of the fir forest advanced almost to the water's edge, their tops like embattled spearpoints against the colored sky. From this shore a spit of sand jutted straight out into the lake. On its extremity, his magnificent bulk and lofty head black against the pellucid orange glow, stood a giant bull-moose, motionless as if modelled in bronze. His huge muzzle was thrust straight out before him, as if he was about to roar a challenge. His wide, palmated antlers were laid back over his shoulders.

Far down the lake a solitary huntsman lay beside a dying camp-fire, and gazed at the splendid silhouette. A faint puff of the aromatic woodsmoke, breathing across his nostrils at that moment, bit the picture into his memory so ineffaceably, that never after could he sniff the smell of wood-smoke on evening air without the desolate splendor of that spacious and shining scene leaping into his brain. But he was a hunter, and the great bull was his quarry. Where he lay he was invisible against the dark background of tree and brush. Presently he reached for his rifle and for a trumpet-like roll of birch bark which lay close by. Noiselessly as a snake he crawled to the shelter of a thicket of young firs. Then he arose to his feet and slipped into the forest.

At the same instant the moose, as if some warning of his unseen foe had been flashed into his consciousness, turned and strode off, without a sound, into the woods.

Soon the tiny camp-fire had died to a few white ashes, and the half-dark of a cloudless night had fallen — still, and chill, and faintly sweet with damp, tonic scents of spruce, bayberry, and bracken. There was that in the air which spoke of frost before morning. It wanted nearly an hour of moonrise. The wide, vague world of the night, that seemed so empty, so unstirring, grew populous with unseen, furtive life — life hunting and hunted; loving, fearing, trembling; enjoying or avenging. But there was no sound, except now and then the inexplicable rustle of a dead leaf, or an elvish gurgle of water from somewhere in the shadows along shore.

At last the hunter, threading his way through the forest as noiselessly as the craftiest of the prowling kindreds, arrived in the heart of a covert of young fir-trees, from beneath whose sweeping branches he could command a near and clear view of the sand-spit. Disappointed he was, but not surprised, to find that the great moose-

bull had disappeared. Seating himself with his
back to a small tree, his rifle and the birch-bark
trumpet, or "moose call," across his knees, he
settled down to wait — to wait with that ex-
haustless patience, that alert yet immobile vigilance, which are, perhaps, hardest to acquire of all
the essentials of woodcraft. In the stillness the
wood-mice came out and resumed their play, with
fairy-thin squeaks and almost inaudible patterings
and rustlings over the dry carpet of the fir needles.

At last, above the flat, black horizon beyond
the lower end of the lake, came the first pale
glow of moonrise. At sight of it the hunter
lifted the birch-bark horn to his lips and breathed
through it a deep, bleating call, grotesque and
wild, yet carrying an indescribable appeal, as if
it were the voice of all the longing of the wilderness. Twice he sounded the uncouth call. Then
he waited, listening, thrilled with exquisite expectancy.

He knew that, when one called a moose, one
never knew what might come. It might, of
course, be the expected bull, his lofty, antlered
head thrusting out over the dark screen of the
bushes, while his burning eyes stared about in
search of the mate to whose longing call he had
hastened. In that case he might perhaps feel
vaguely that he had been deceived, and fall back

soundlessly into the darkness; or, taking it into his head that another bull had forestalled him, he might burst out into the open, shaking his antlers, thrashing the bushes, and roaring savage challenge. But, on the other hand, it might not be a bull at all that would come to the lying summons. It might be an ungainly moose-cow, mad with jealousy and frantically resolved to trample her rival beneath her knife-edged hoofs. Or it might be something dangerously different. It might be a bear, a powerful old male, who had learned to spring upon a cow-moose and break her neck with one stroke of his armed paw. In such a contingency there was apt to be excitement; for when a bear undertakes to stalk a cow-moose, he gives no notice of his intentions. The first warning, then, of his approach, would be his final savage rush upon the utterer of the lying call. For such a contingency the hunter held his rifle always ready.

But, on the other hand, there might well be nothing at all — no answer, all through the long, cold, moon-silvered night, summon the birch horn never so craftily.

And this was what the hunter thought had been so far the result of his calling. Had he chanced to look over his shoulder, he might have known better. He might have seen the shadows take substance, condensing into a gigantic and solid bulk just behind the little tree against which he leaned his back. He might have seen the spread of vast and shadowy antlers, the long, sullen head, and drooping muzzle, the little eyes, in which, as they detected him in his ambush, a sudden flame of rage was quenched by the timely wisdom of fear. But the giant shape dissolved back into shadow, and the hunter never knew that he himself had been stalked and considered.

After a long silence, the birch-bark horn again sent forth its appeal. Loud and long it called; then it murmured a series of caressingly desirous notes, impatient and importunate. When it stopped, from the thick dark just below the sand-spit came a light snapping of twigs and brushing of branches, which seemed to be moving toward the open point. The hunter was puzzled; for a moose-bull, coming in answer to the call, would either come with a defiant rush, and make a much louder noise, or he would come secretively and make no noise whatever. With pounding pulses he leaned forward to see what would emerge upon the sand-spit.

To his surprise, it was no moose, but a small gray caribou cow, looking almost white in the level rays of the now half-risen moon. She was followed by another cow, larger and darker than the first, and then by a fine caribou bull. Softly, alluringly, the hunter sounded his call again, but not one of the caribou paid any attention to it whatever. To the bull of the caribou it mattered not what lovelorn cow-moose should voice her hoarse appeals to the moon. He and his followers were on their own affairs intent.

He was a noble specimen of his kind, as to stature, with a very light grayish head, neck, and shoulders, showing white in contrast to the dull brown of the rest of his coat. But his antlers, though large, were unevenly developed, so obviously imperfect that the hunter, who wanted heads, not hides or meat, hesitated to shoot. He chose rather to bide his time, and hope for a more perfect specimen, the law of New Brunswick allowing him only one.

For several minutes the bull stood staring across the lake, as though half minded to swim it, and his two cows — antlered like himself, though much less imposingly — watched him with dutiful attention. Whatever his purpose, however, it was never declared ; for suddenly there came a new and more impetuous crashing among the undergrowth, and the eyes of the little herd turned to see what was approaching. An instant later a second bull, about the size of the first, but very much darker in coloring, broke furiously through the bushes. He rushed about half-way down the sand-spit, then stopped, snorting and blowing defiance.

The new-comer had a magnificent set of antlers, but the hunter forgot to shoot.

The white bull, surprised by the unexpected challenge, stood for an instant staring stupidly, waving his great ears. Then all at once the hot blood of arrogant possession and jealous mastery seemed to rush to his head. Thrusting aside the two cows, who stood huddled in his path, with a furious booing grunt, he lurched forward to meet the challenger.

With lowered heads, noses between their knees, and the branching spikes of their antlers presented straight to the front, they came together with a shock and a snort. The hard horn clashed with the dry resonance of seasoned wood. Being of about equal size, both withstood the shock. Both staggered ; but, recovering themselves instantly, they stood pushing with all the strength of their straining, heaving bodies, their hoofs digging deep into the sand.

Then, on a sudden, as if the same idea had at the same instant flashed into both their seething brains, they disengaged and jumped backward, like wary fencers.

For several tense seconds they stood eying

each other, antlers down, while the big-eyed cows, with ears slowly waving, looked on placidly, and the moon, now full risen, flooded the whole scene with lavish radiance. The only concern of the cows was that the best bull should win, with proved mastery compelling their allegiance.

Suddenly the new-comer, the dark bull, as if to get around his adversary's guard, feinted to the right, and then lunged straight forward. But the white bull was too experienced to be caught by such a well-worn ruse. He met the attack fairly. Again the antlers clashed. Again those monstrous pantings and savage gruntings arose on the stillness, as the matched antagonists heaved and pushed, their hind legs straddled awkwardly and their hoofs ploughing the sand.

At length the white bull put one of his hind feet in a hole. Giving way for a second, he was forced backwards almost to the water's edge. With a furious effort, however, he recovered himself, and even, by some special good fortune or momentary slackness of his adversary, regained his lost ground. Both paused for breath. The fight hung exactly in the balance.

To judge from his antlers, the white bull was the older, and therefore, one may suppose, the craftier duellist. It occurred to him now, perhaps, that against a foe so nearly his equal in strength he must seek some advantage in strategy. He made a sudden movement to disengage his antlers and jump aside. To the trained eyes of the hunter, watching from the thicket, the intention was obvious. But it failed curiously. At the very instant of the effort to disengage, the dark bull had surged forward with violence. Not meeting the resistance expected, he was taken by surprise and stumbled to his knees. The white bull, quick to feel his advantage, instantly changed his purpose and surged forward with all his force. For a moment the dark bull seemed to crumple up as his rival's heaving shoulders towered above him.

Now, this was the white bull's chance. It was for him to roll his enemy over, disengage, rip the dark bull's unfortunate flank, and tread him down into the sand. But he did nothing of the sort. He himself staggered forward with the fall of his adversary. Then he drew back again, but slowly. With the motion his adversary regained his feet. Once more the two stood, armed front to front, grunting, straining, sweating, heaving, but neither giving ground an inch.

"Locked!" said the hunter, under his breath.

That, indeed, was the fact. The two pairs of antlers were interlaced. But the sinister truth was not yet realized by the combatants themselves, because, when either tried to back free, so as to renew the attack more advantageously, it seemed to him quite natural that the other should furiously follow him up. In the confused struggle that now followed, they more than once pivoted completely around; and the two cows, perceiving something unusual in the combat, drew off with a disapproving air to the extremity of the sandspit. Little by little the white bull appeared to be getting a shade the better of the duel; for at length, regaining his first position, he began forcing his rival steadily, though slowly, back toward the woods. Then all at once, during a pause for breath, both at the same moment awoke to knowledge of the plight they had got themselves into. Both had sought to back away at the same instant. In the next they were tugging frantically to break apart.

But struggle as they might their efforts were utterly in vain. The tough, strong horn of their new antlers was ever so slightly elastic. It had yielded, under the impact of their last charge, just far enough for a perfect locking. But in the opposite direction there was no yielding. They were inextricably and inexorably fixed together, and in a horrid attitude, in which it was impossible to feed, or even to straighten up their bowed necks.

In the agonized pulling match which now began, the white bull had the best of it. He had slightly the advantage in weight. Little by little he dragged his grunting rival out along the sandspit, till the two cows, almost crowded off, bounced past with indignant snorts and vanished down the shore. A moment more, and he had backed off the sand into a couple of feet of water.

The shock of the plunge seemed to startle the white bull into new rage. He laid the blame of it upon his foe. As if with all his strength renewed, he recovered himself, and thrust the dark bull backward with such tempestuous force that the latter had all he could do to keep his footing. Presently he felt himself at the edge of the woods, his hind feet in a tangle of bushes instead of on the sand. Then, exhausted and cowed, his legs gave way, and he sank back upon his haunches. Frantic with despair, he struggled to butt and strike with his fettered prongs, and in this futile struggle he fell over on his side. The white bull, his paroxysm of new vigor come suddenly to an end, was dragged down with him, and the two lay with heaving flanks, panting noisily.

The hunter had laid down his roll of birch bark. He was just about to step forth from his ambush and mercifully end the matter with his knife. But there came a brusque intervention. He had not been the only spectator of the strange combat.

Out from the thickets at the lower edge of the point came plunging an enormous black bear. With one huge paw uplifted, he fell upon the exhausted duellists. One blow smashed the neck of the white bull. Turning to the other, who glared up at him with rolling, hopeless eyes, he fell to biting at him with slow, luxurious cruelty.

In that instant the hunter's rifle blazed from the thicket. The bear, shot through the spine with an explosive bullet, dropped in a sprawling heap across the bent forelegs of his victim. Stepping forth into the moonlight, the hunter drew his knife with precision across the throat of the wounded bull.

Straightening himself up, he stared for a few moments at the three great lifeless carcasses on the sand. Then he let his glance sweep out over the glassy waters and level, desolate shores. How strange was the sudden silence, the still white peace of the moonlight, after all that madness and tumult and rage which had just been so abruptly stilled! A curious revulsion of feeling all at once blotted out his triumph, and there came over him a sense of repugnance to the bulk of so much death. Stepping around it, he sat down with his back to it all, on a stranded log, and proceeded to fill his pipe.

F

THE SENTRY OF THE
SEDGE-FLATS

The Sentry of the Sedge-Flats

PALE, shimmering green, and soaked in sun, the miles of sedge-flats lay outspread from the edges of the slow bright water to the foot of the far, dark-wooded, purple hills. Winding through the quiet green levels came a tranquil little stream. Where its sleepy current joined the great parent river, a narrow tongue of bare sand jutted out into the golden-glowing water. At the extreme tip of the sand-spit towered, sentry-like, a long-legged gray-blue bird, as motionless as if he had been transplanted thither from the panel of a Japanese screen.

The flat narrow head of the great heron, with its long, javelin-like, yellow beak and two slender black crest-feathers, was drawn far back by a curious undulation of the immensely long neck, till it rested between the humped blue wing-shoulders. From the lower part of the neck hung a fine fringe of vaporous rusty-gray plumes, which lightly veiled the chestnut-colored breast. The bird might have seemed asleep, like the drowsy expanses of green sedge, silver-blue water, and opalescent turquoise sky, but for its eyes. Those eyes, round, unwinking, of a hard, glassy gold with intense black pupils, were unmistakably and savagely wide awake.

Over the tops of the sedges, fluttering and zigzagging waywardly, came a big butterfly, its gorgeous red-brown wings pencilled with strange hieroglyphs in black and purple. It danced out a little way over the water; and then, as if suddenly terrified by the shining peril beneath, came wavering back toward shore. A stone's throw up the channel of the little stream lay a patch of vivid green, the leaves of the arrow-weed, with its delicate, pallid blooms dreaming in the still air above them. The butterfly saw these blossoms, or perhaps smelt them, and fluttered in their direction to see if those pure chalices held honey. But on his way he noted the moveless figure of the heron, conspicuous above the ranks of the sedge. Perhaps he took the curious shape for a post or a stump. In any case, it seemed to offer an alluring place of rest, where he might pause for a moment and flaunt his glowing wings in the sun before dancing onward to the honey-blossoms. He flickered nearer. To him those unwinking jewels of eyes had no menace. He hovered an instant about two feet above them. In that instant, like a flash of light, the long, pale neck and straight yellow beak shot out; and the butter-

fly was caught neatly. Twisting his head shoreward, without shifting his feet, the heron struck
the glowing velvet wings of the insect sharply on
the sand. Then, having swallowed the morsel
leisurely, he drew his head down again between
his shoulders, and resumed his moveless waiting.

The next matter of interest to come within the
vision of those inscrutable eyes was a dragon-fly
chase. Hurtling low over the sedge-tops, and
flashing in the sunlight like a lace-pin of rubies,
came a small rose-colored dragon-fly, fleeing for
its life before a monster of its species which blazed
in emerald and amethyst. The chase could have
but one ending, for the giant had the speed as
well as the voracious hunger. The glistening
films of his wings rustled crisply as he overtook
the shining fugitive and caught its slender body
in his jaws. The silver wings of the victim vi-
brated wildly. The chase came to a hovering
pause just before that immobile shape on the
point of the sand-spit. Again the long yellow
beak darted forth. And the radiant flies, captive
and captor together, disappeared.

But such flimsy fare as even the biggest of
butterflies and dragon-flies was not contenting to
the sharp appetite of the heron. He took one
stiff-legged stride forward, and stood in about six
inches of water. Here he settled himself in a

somewhat altered position, his back more awkwardly hunched, his head held lower, and his dagger of a bill pointing downward. His wicked
golden eyes were not indifferent to the possibilities
of the air above him, but they were now concern-
ing themselves more particularly with the water
which flowed about his feet.

If any one stands at the brink of a quiet summer stream, and keeps still enough, and watches
intently enough, however deserted the landscape
may appear, he will see life in many furtive forms
go by. The great blue heron kept still enough.
The water at this point went softly over a shoal
half sand, half mud, and in the faint movement
of the clear amber-brown current the sunlight
wove a shimmering network on the bottom.
Across this darted a shadow. The heron's beak
shot downward with an almost inaudible splash,
transfixing the shadow, and emerged with a glittering green and silver perch, perhaps five inches
in length. The quivering body of the fish had
its knife-edged gills wide open, and every spine
of its formidable, armed fins threateningly erect.
But the triumphant fisherman strode ashore with
it and proceeded to hammer it into unconscious-
ness on the hard sand. Then he swallowed it
head first, thus effectually disarming every weapon
of fin and gill-cover. The progress of this sub-

stantial mouthful could be traced clearly down the
bird's slim length of gullet, accompanied as it was
by several seconds of contortions so violent that
they made the round yellow eyes wink gravely.
As soon as the morsel was fairly down the bird
stretched its neck to its full length, with a curious
hitch of the base as if to assure himself the process was completed.   Then he resumed his post
of watching.   He had no more than taken his
place than a huge black tadpole wriggled by over
the gold-meshed bottom.   It was speared and
swallowed in an eye-wink.   Soft, slippery, and
spineless, it made but a moment's incident.

A little after, on the smooth surface of the
smaller stream, some fifty feet up-channel, a tiny
ripple appeared.   Swiftly it drew near.   It was
pointed, and with a long fine curve of oily ripple
trailing back from it on either side, like the outline of a comet's tail.   As it approached, in the
apex of the parabola could be seen a minute black
nose, with two bright, dark little eyes just behind
it.   It was a small water-rat, voyaging adventur-
ously out from its narrow inland haunts among
the lilies.

The great heron eyed its approach.   To the
swimmer, no doubt, the blue-gray, immobile
shape at the extremity of the sand-spit looked like
some weather-beaten post, placed there by man

for his inexplicable convenience in regard to
hitching boats. But presently, something strange
in the shape of the post seemed to strike the little
voyager's attention. He stopped. Perhaps he
saw the menacing glitter of that yellow, unwinking stare. After a moment of wavering irresolution, he changed his course, swam straight across
channel, scrambled out upon the wet mud of the
farther shore, and vanished among the pale root-
stalks of the sedge. The heron was savage with
disappointment; but no slightest movement be-
trayed his anger, save that the pinkish film of the
lower lid blinked up once, as it were with a snap,
over each implacable eye. His time would come
— which faith is that which supports all those
who know how to wait. He peered upstream
for the coming of another and less wary water-rat.

Instead of the expected ripple, however, he
now caught sight of a shadow which flickered
across the surface of the water and in an instant
had vanished over the pale sea of the grass-tops.
He looked up. In the blue above hung poised,
his journeying flight just at that moment arrested,
a wide-winged duck-hawk, boldest marauder of
the air. The heron threw his head far back, till
his beak pointed straight skyward. At the same
time he half lifted his strong wings, poising himself to deliver a thrust with all the strength that

was in him. On the instant the hawk dropped like a wedge of steel out of the sky, his rigid, half-closed pinions hissing with the speed of his descent. The heron never flinched. But within ten feet of him the hawk, having no mind to impale himself on that waiting spear-point, opened his wings, swerved upward, and went past with a harsh hum of wing-feathers. Wheeling again, almost instantly, he swooped back to the attack, buffeting the air just above the heron's head, but taking care not to come within range of the deadly beak. The heron refused to be drawn from his position of effective defence, and made no movement except to keep the point of his lance ever toward the foe. And presently the hawk, seeing the futility of his assaults, winged off sullenly to hunt for some unwary duck or gosling.

As he went the heron stretched himself to his full gaunt height and stared after him in triumph. Then, turning his head slowly, he scanned the whole expanse of windless grass and sunlit water. One sight fixed his attention. Far up the windings of the lesser stream he marked a man in a boat. The man was not rowing, but sitting in the stern and propelling the boat noiselessly with an Indian paddle. From time to time he halted and examined the shore minutely. Once in a while, after such an examination, he would get out, kneel down, and be occupied for several minutes among the weeds of the shallows along the stream's edge. He was looking at the musquash holes in the bank, and setting traps before those which showed signs of present occupancy. The heron watched the process, unstirring as a dead stump, till he thought the man was coming too near. Then, spreading a vast, dark pair of wings, he rose indignantly and flapped heavily away up river, trailing his length of black legs just over the sedge-tops.

Not far above the mouth of the stream the man set the last of his musquash traps. Then he paddled back leisurely by the way he had come, his dingy yellow straw hat appearing to sail close over the grass as the boat followed the windings of the stream. When the yellow hat had at length been swallowed up in the violet haze along the base of the uplands, the great blue heron reappeared, winging low along the river shore. Arriving at the sand-spit he dropped his feet to the shallow water, closed his wings, and settled abruptly into a rigid pose of watching, with his neck outstretched and his head held high in the air.

The most searching scrutiny revealed nothing in all the tranquil summer landscape to disturb him. Nevertheless, he seemed to have lost conceit of his sentry post on the tip of the sand-spit. Instead of settling down to watch for what might come to him, he decided to go and look for what he wanted. With long, ungainly, precise, but absolutely noiseless strides, he took his slow way up along the shore of the little river, walking on the narrow margin of mud between the grass-roots and the water. As he went his long neck undulated sinuously at each stride, his head was held low, and his eyes glared under every drooping leaf. The river margin, both in the water and out of it, was populous with insect life and the darting bill took toll of it at every step. But the most important game was frogs. There were plenty of them, small, greenish ochre fellows, who sat on the lily leaves and stared with foolish goggle-eyes till that stalking blue doom was almost upon them. Then they would dive head-foremost into the water, quick almost as the fleeting of a shadow. But quicker still was the stroke of the yellow beak — and the captive, pounded into limpness, would vanish down his captor's insatiable throat. This was better hunting than he had had upon the sand-spit, and he followed it up with great satisfaction. He even had the triumph of capturing a small water-rat, which had darted out of the grass-roots just as he came by.

The little beast was tenacious of life, and had to
be well hammered on the mud before it would
consent to lie still enough to be swallowed comfortably. This pleasant task, however, was presently accomplished; and the great bird, as he
stretched his head upward to give his neck that
final hitch which drove the big mouthful home,
took a careless step backward into the shallow
water. There was a small sinister sound, and
something closed relentlessly on his leg. He
had stepped into a steel trap.

Stung by the sharp pain, astounded by the
strangeness of the attack, and panic-stricken, as
all wild creatures are by the sudden forfeit of their
freedom, the great bird lost all his dignified self-
possession. First he nearly broke his beak with
mad jabs at the inexplicable horror that had
clutched him. Then, with a hoarse squawk of
terror, he went quite wild. His huge wings flapped
frantically, beating down the sedges and the blossoms of the arrow-weed, as he struggled to wrench
himself free. He did succeed in lifting the trap
above water; but it was securely anchored, and
after a minute or two of insane, convulsive effort,
it dragged him down again. Again and again he
lifted it; again and yet again it dragged him
down inexorably. And so the blind battle went
on, with splashing of water and heavy buffeting

of wings, till at last the bird fell back utterly
beaten. In the last bout the trap had turned and
got itself wedged in a slanting position, so that it
was impossible for the captive to hold himself up-
right. He lay sprawling on his thighs, one wing
outspread over the mud and leaves, the other on
the water. His deadly beak was half open, from
exhaustion. Only his indomitable eyes, still
round, gold-and-black, glittering like gems,
showed no sign of his weakness or his fear.

For a long time he lay there motionless, half
numbed by the sense of defeat and by that gnawing anguish in his leg. Unheeded, the gleaming
dragon-flies hurtled and darted, flashed and poised
quivering, just above his head. Unheeded, the
yellow butterflies, and the pale blue butterflies,
alighted near him on the blooms of the arrow-
weed. A big green bull-frog swam up and
clambered out upon the mud close before him —
to catch sight at once of that bright, terrible eye
and fall back into the water almost paralyzed
with fright; but still he made no movement.
His world had fallen about him, and there was
nothing for him to do but wait and see what
would happen next — what shape his doom
would take.

Meanwhile, down along the margin mud, still
hidden from view by a bend of the stream, an-

other stealthy hunter was approaching. The big brown mink, who lived far upstream in a musk-rat hole whose occupants he had cornered and devoured, was out on one of his foraging expeditions. Nothing in the shape of flesh, fish, or insect came amiss to him; but having ever the blood-lust in his ferocious veins, so that he loved to slaughter even when his appetite was well sated, he preferred, of course, big game — something that could struggle, and suffer, and give him the sense of killing. A nesting duck or plover, for example, or a family of musquash — that was something worth while. On this day he had caught nothing but insects and a few dull frogs. He was savage for red blood.

Very short in the legs, but extraordinarily long in the body, lithe, snake-like in his swift darting movements, every inch of him a bundle of tough elastic muscles, with a sharp triangular head and incredibly malevolent eyes, the mink was a figure to be dreaded by creatures many times his size. As he came round the bend of the stream, and saw the great blue bird lying at the water's edge with wings outstretched, the picture of helplessness, his eyes glowed suddenly like live coals blown upon. He ran forward without an instant's hesitation, and made as if to spring straight at the captive's throat.

This move, however, was but a feint; for the big mink, though his knowledge of herons was by no means complete, knew nevertheless that the heron's beak was a weapon to beware of. He swerved suddenly, sprang lightly to one side, and tried to close in from the rear. But he didn't know the flexibility of the heron's neck. The lightning rapidity of his attack almost carried it through; but not quite. He was met by a darting stroke of the great yellow beak, which hurled him backward and ploughed a deep red furrow across his shoulder. Before he could recover himself the bird's neck was coiled again like a set spring, the javelin beak poised for another blow.

Most of the wild creatures would have been discouraged by such a reception, and slunk away to look for easier hunting. But not so the mink. His fighting blood now well up, for him it was a battle to the death. But for all his rage he did not lose his cunning. Making as if to run away, he doubled upon himself with incredible swiftness and flew at his adversary's neck. Quick as he was, however, he could not be so quick as that miracle of speed, which the eye can scarcely follow, the heron's thrust. The blow caught him this time on the flank, but slantingly, leaving a terrible gash, and at the same time a lucky buffet

G

from the elbow of one great wing dashed him into the water. With this success the heron strove to rise to his feet — a position from which he could have fought to greater advantage. But the lay of the trap pulled him down again irresistibly. As he sank back the mink clambered out upon the shore and crouched straight in front of him, just a little beyond the reach of his stroke.

The mink was now a picture of battle fury, every muscle quivering, blood pulsing from his gashes, his white teeth showing in a soundless snarl, his eyes seeming to throb with crimson fire. The heron, on the other hand, seemed absolutely composed. His head, immobile, alert, in perfect readiness, was drawn back between his shoulders. His eyes were as wide, and fixed, and clear, and glassily staring, as the jewelled eyes of an idol.

For some seconds the mink crouched, as if trying to stare his adversary out of countenance. Then he launched himself straight at the bird's back. The movement had all the impetuosity of a genuine attack, but with marvellous control it was checked on the instant. It had been enough, however, to draw the heron's counter-stroke, which fell just short of its object. With the bird's recovery the mink shot in to close quarters. He received a second blow, which laid open the side of his face, but it was a short stroke, with not enough force behind it to repulse him. Ignoring it, he closed, fixed his teeth in the bird's neck, and flung his lithe length over the back, where it would be out of reach of the buffeting wings.

The battle was over; for the mink's teeth were long and strong. They cut deep, straight into the life; and, undisturbed by the windy flopping of the great, helpless wings, the victor lay drinking the life-blood which he craved. A black whirling shadow sailed over the scene, but it passed a little behind the mink's tail and was not noticed. It paused, seeming to hover over a patch of lily leaves. A moment more, and it vanished. There was a hiss; and the great duck-hawk, the same one whom the heron had driven off earlier in the day, dropped out of the zenith. The mink had just time to raise his snarling and dripping muzzle in angry surprise when the hawk's talons closed upon him. One set fastened upon his throat, cutting straight through windpipe and jugular; the other set gripped and pierced his tender loins. The next moment he was jerked from the body of his prey, and carried — head, legs, and tail limply hanging — away far over the green wastes of the sedge to the great hawk's eyrie, in the heart

of the cedar-swamp beyond the purple uplands.

Some ten minutes later a splendid butterfly, all
glowing orange and maroon, came and settled on
the back of the dead heron, and waved its radiant
wings in the tranquil light.

A TREE-TOP AERONAUT

A Tree-Top Aeronaut

ALTHOUGH in the open clearings it was full noon — the noon of early September, hot and blue and golden — here in the lofty aisles of the forest it was all cold twilight. Such light as glimmered down through the thick-leaved tree-tops was of a mellow shadowy brown and a translucent green, changing from the one tone to the other mysteriously as the eye shifted its backgrounds. One tall trunk, long ago shattered and broken off just below the crown by a stroke of lightning, stood pointing bleakly toward a round opening in the leafy roof, reaching upward a thin-foliaged, half-dead, gnarled and twisted arm.

In the outer shell and coarse strong bark of the stricken tree life lingered tenaciously, but its heart was fallen to decay. Near the base of the arm a round hole gave entrance, through the shell of live wood, to a chamber in the hollow heart. The chamber had yet another entrance, beneath a knot, higher up on the opposite side of the trunk. Through these two holes filtered a dim warm light, just strong enough to show a huddle of small, ruddy-brown, furry shapes sleeping snugly at the bottom of the chamber.

The forest was as still and soundless as a dream, under the spell of the noonday heat. But presently the silence was broken by the approach of heavy footsteps, now crackling as they crunched the dry twigs, now muffled and dull as they sank into beds of deep moss. They were plainly human footsteps, for no other creature but man would move so crudely and heedlessly through the forest quiet. Every one of the wild kindred, from the bear down to the wood-mouse, would move with a furtive wariness, desiring always to see without being seen, either intent upon some hunting or solicitous to avoid some hunter.

Down a shadowy corridor of soaring trunks came into view two figures — a tall heavy-shouldered lumberman, carrying an axe, and a slim boy with a light rifle in his hand. It was the lumberman, booted and long-striding, who made all the noise. The boy, in moccasins, stepped lightly as an Indian, his eager blue eyes searching every nook and stump and branch as he went, hoping at every step to surprise some secret of the furtive wood-folk.

Near the foot of the blasted tree he stopped, looking up.

" I wonder what lives in that hole up there, Jabe ? " he said.

The lumberman peered upward critically.

"Jiminy, ef that ain't a likely-lookin' squir'l tree ! " he answered.

" Squirrel tree ! " echoed the boy. " As if every tree wasn't a squirrel tree, wherever there's a squirrel 'round ! "

" Aye, but there's squir'ls an' squir'ls ! You'll see ! " retorted the woodsman ; and, swinging his axe, he brought the back of it down upon the trunk in three or four sounding strokes.

Straightway a dark little shape, appearing in the hole beneath the branch, launched itself into the air. It looked like a leap of des- peration, as there was no tree within reach of any ordinary quadruped's leap. Yet the daring little shape was plainly that of a quadruped, not of a bird. It was followed instantly, in lightning succession, by six or seven others equally daring ; and all went sailing away, in different directions, across the mysteriously shadowed air. They sailed on long downward slants, with legs spread wide apart and connected on each side by furry membrane, so that they looked like some kind of grotesque, oblong toy umbrellas broken loose in a breeze. The boy stared after them with an exclamation of wonder and delight, trying to keep his eye on them all at once; but in a moment they had disappeared, gaining the shelter of other trees, and effacing themselves from view as if by enchantment.

All but one. As the flying squirrels came aeroplaning from their rudely assaulted citadel, the woodsman had dropped his axe, snatched up a bit of stick about a foot long, and hurled it after one of the gliding figures. Your woodsman is an unerring shot with the hurled axe, the pike-pole, or the billet of wood; but up there, in the deceitful transparency of shadow and glimmer, the little aeronaut was sailing with an elusive speed. The whirling missile almost missed its mark. It just caught the outspread furry tail, which was serving as a rudder and balancer to that adventurous flight. The tail, tough and flexible, gave way and took no injury. But the tiny aeroplanist, his balance rudely destroyed, plunged headlong to the ground.

"Oh-h-h!" exclaimed the boy, with long-drawn commiseration. But, his curiosity too strong for his pity, he raced forward with the woodsman to capture and examine their prize.

There was no prize to be found. Both had seen the flier come to earth. Both had marked, with expert eyes, the exact point of his fall. But there was nothing to be seen but a softly disappearing dent in the cushion of moss.

"Well, I'll be — jiggered!" said the woodsman, fingering his stubbled chin and scrutinizing the nearest tree-trunks with narrowed eyes.

"Serves us right!" said the boy. "I'm glad he's got away. I thought you'd killed him, Jabe!"

"Reckon I just *blowed* him over," responded the woodsman. "But now ye know where they hang out, ye kin ketch one alive in a cage-trap, if ye want to git to know somethin' of his manners an' customs — eh, what? When ye've *killed* one of these wild critters, after all, to my mind he ain't no more interestin' than a lady's fur boa."

As the two man creatures disappeared down the confusing vistas of the forest, the soft dark eyes of the flying-squirrel, disproportionately large and prominent, with a vagueness of depth which made them seem all pupil, stared after them mildly from the refuge of a high crotched branch. Unhurt, even unbewildered by his dizzy plunge, he had bounced aside with a motion too swift for his enemies' eyes to follow, and placed a tree-trunk between himself and peril. Darting up the trunk like a fleeting brown streak, he had been safely hidden before his enemies reached the tree.

In his high retreat, the flying-squirrel did not

crouch as a red squirrel would have done, but lay
stretched and spread out as if flattened by violence
upon the bark. His color, of an obscure warm
brown, faintly smudged with a darker tone, blended
so perfectly with the hue of the bark that, if the
eye once looked away, it could with difficulty
detect him again. A member of a little-known
branch of the flying-squirrel family, — the flying-
squirrel of Eastern Canada, — he was nearly a foot
in length, some two inches longer than the common flying-squirrel, from whom he differed also
very sharply in color, his retiring brown and
gray being in marked contrast to the buff and
drab and pure white of his lesser but more famous
cousin. Buff and white would have been so conspicuous a livery in the brown Canadian forests
that his ancestors would never have survived to
produce him had they not managed to change that
livery in time to baffle their foes.

The flying-squirrel, unlike the impudent and
irrepressible red squirrel, had a great capacity for
patience, as well as for prudence. Moreover, he
had no great liking for activity as long as the sun
was up, his enormous eyes adapting him for the
dim life of the night. For some minutes after the
sound of footsteps had died away in the distance,
he lay unstirring on his branch, his ears alert to
the tiniest forest whisper, his nostrils quivering as

they interrogated every subtlest forest scent. All at once his wide eyes grew even wider, and a sort of spasm of apprehension flitted across their liquid depths. What was that faint, dry, rustling sound —the mere ghost of a whisper — on the bark of the trunk behind him? Nervously he turned his head. There was nothing in sight, but the ghostly sound continued, so slight, so thin, that even his fine ear could hardly be sure of its reality.

The little watcher remained moveless as a knot on the bark. The creeping whisper softly mounted the tree. Then at last a flat, brownish-black, vicious head came into view around the trunk, and arrested itself, swaying softly, just over the base of the branch. It was the head of a large black snake.

The snake's eyes, dull yet deadly, met those of the squirrel and held them. For a moment the black head was rigid. Then it began to sway again, with a slow hypnotizing motion. The eyes — shallow, opaque, venomous — seemed to draw closer together as they concentrated their energy upon the mildly glowing orbs of their intended victim. At last the waving head began to draw near, the black body undulating stealthily into view behind it. Nearer, nearer it came, the flat hard eyes never shifting, till it seemed that one lightning lunge would have enabled it to fix its fangs in the fascinated victim's neck. But at this moment the little aeronaut whisked half round, flirted his broad fluff of a tail straight out behind him, and sailed quietly from his perch on a long gradual swoop, which brought him back to the base of the tree from which he had originally started. The hypnotizing experiment of the black snake had been, in this instance, an unqualified failure. Angry and disappointed, the snake withdrew to hunt mice or other easier game. The flying-squirrel ran cheerfully up the tree, slipped back into the hole, and curled himself up complacently to sleep away the rest of the daylight. Of his companions, two had already stealthily returned, and the others crept in soon afterwards quite unruffled.

That night moonrise came to the forest close on the vanishing trail of the sunset. A long white ray, flooding in through the tree-tops, lit up the hole beneath the branch of the blasted trunk. Without haste the flying-squirrels came one after another to their high doorway and launched themselves upon the still air. One might have thought that their first purpose would have been to forage for a meal; but, instead of that, they seemed like children just let out of school, bent on nothing so much as relieving their pent-up spirits. Probably they were not hungry. It was the season of abundance, and they had, perhaps, ample store of green nuts and tender young pine-cones within their hollow tree. In any case, they knew the forest was full of good provender for them, the forest-floor covered with berries for when they should choose to descend and gather them. There was no hurry. It was good to amuse themselves in their high and dim-lit world.

Their favorite game seemed to be to criss-cross each other, as it were, in their long gliding flights, which, beginning near the top of one tree would end generally near the foot of another, as far away as the impetus of their start and their descent would allow. Thence they would dart nimbly to the top again, sometimes with a restrained *chirr* of mirth, to repeat the gay ad-venture. Sometimes, when their descent was steep, they would rise again toward the end of it, by altering, probably, the angle of their mem-branes or side-planes. As they flashed spectrally past each other, touched suddenly by some white finger of moonlight, their play was like an aerial game of tag. But they never actually " tagged " each other. Most likely they took good care to avoid any approach to contact in mid flight, which might have meant a fall to the dangerous forest-floor, the haunt of prowling foxes, skunks, and weasels.

But though their chief dread seemed to be of the far dark ground and its perils, there were perils, too, for the little aeronauts even in their leafy heights. In the midst of their leaping, gliding, and sailing, there came a hollow cry across the tree-tops. It was a melancholy sound but full of menace — a *whoo-hoo-hoo-oo-oo* — repeated at long, uncertain, nerve-racking intervals. It sounded remote enough from the hollow tree, but at its first note the game of the furry aeroplanists came to a stop. One would have said that there were no such things as flying-squirrels in the Quah-Davic woods.

After some fifteen or twenty minutes of sepulchral summons and answer, the calling of the owls ceased. In perhaps fifteen minutes more, the flying-squirrels seemed to make up their minds that the danger had removed to some other part of the forest. Then, at first timorously, but soon with all their former merriment and zest, the tree-top aeronauts resumed their game.

The game was at its height. Down a long aisle of the forest the high moon poured a flood of unobstructed light. Athwart this lane of brilliance the flying-squirrels went passing and repassing. On a sudden, as one of them was sailing gayly across, it was as if a fragment of black cloud fell upon him noiselessly out of the whiteness, blotting him out. Somewhere in the cloud burned two terrible round eyes, and beneath it reached forth two sets of rending talons. The life of the gay little glider was clutched out of him with a strangled scream, and the cloudy shape, its eyes blazing coldly, drifted away into the shadows with its prey.

The game came to a full stop — for that night at the least. As luck would have it, the squirrel who had been through the adventures of the morning — the encounter with Jabe Smith's missile and the interview with that would-be mesmerizer, the black snake — had been sailing just below his unhappy playmate at the moment of the great wood-owl's swoop. He had seen the whole tragedy, and it made him distrustful of aeroplaning for the moment. He decided to emulate his cousin the red squirrel, and trust to running and climbing, to the solid trunks and branches, rather than to the treacheries of the air. After hiding in a crotch till his palpitations had somewhat calmed down, he descended the tree in a cautious search for food. He had had his fill of nuts and cones; he wanted juicier fare. He went on all the way down to earth, his appetite set on the ripening partridge-berries.

Now, as it chanced, the boy had taken to heart that suggestion of the lumberman's in regard to the

ч

cage-trap. His appetite for knowledge of all the
wild creatures of the woods was insatiable. He was
eager to know the flying-squirrels more intimately
than he could know them from the plates and text
of his natural history books. His idea was to catch
one, keep it a while, win its confidence, study it,
and then give it back its freedom before it had
time to forget how to take care of itself among
the perils of freedom. That very afternoon,
therefore, he had returned to the "squirr'l tree,"
carrying a spacious trap-cage of strong wire — a
cage of two chambers, in which he had already
kept with success both red squirrels and ground
squirrels. The second or inner chamber was the
regulation revolving wire cylinder, designed to
give the little captive such strenuous exercise as it
might crave, and to divert its thoughts from its
captivity. The door was a wide trap, opening
upwards and outwards, and shutting with a powerful spring at the least touch upon the trigger
within. Beyond the trigger the boy had fixed a
varied bait, cunningly calculated to the vagaries
of the squirrel appetite. There were sweet nut-
kernels securely tied down, a fragrant piece of
apple, a bit of green corn-ear, and a crisp morsel
of bacon rind.

The boy had no means of knowing whether
the flying-squirrel was like his red cousin or not

in the matter of a taste for meat. But he felt sure that some one or another of these scented dainties would prove too much for the prudence of anything that called itself a squirrel. Near the great trunk of the blasted tree he found another giant, half fallen, its top still upheld by the embrace of its stout-armed neighbors. The long gradual incline he rightly judged to be a favorite pathway of the flying-squirrels as they raced upwards from their excursions to the forest floor. So, upon the slope of the trunk, some six or seven feet above the earth, he fixed his trap securely, and left it to show what it could do.

For a long time, however, it did nothing. It was a new strange thing on the familiar path, and all the little people of the wild avoided it. Till near the first gray of dawn not a flying-squirrel had dared approach its neighborhood.

The forest powers seem to have sometimes a mischievous trick of selecting some particular one of their children for special trial, of following up that one for days with a kind of persecution. So it came about that the same adventurous little aeronaut who had fallen foul of both Jabe Smith and the black snake, and had so narrowly escaped the pounce of the brown owl, had the misfortune to be sighted, as he was feasting on the partridge-

berries not far from the sloping tree, by a weasel
which had had bad luck in his night's hunting.

Sinuous as a snake and swifter, his cruel eyes
glowing like points of live flame, the long yellow
form of the weasel darted forward. With a faint
squeak of terror the squirrel sprang for the sloping trunk, his own hope being to get high enough
to launch himself into the air. But the flying-
squirrel is less nimble on his feet than the red or
the gray. He was much slower than the weasel.
He gained the sloping trunk, indeed, but the foe
was almost at his heels. It looked as if the doom
of the wild was upon him. By a frantic effort,
however, he evaded for a second the weasel's rush.
Desperately he raced up the well-known trail. He
came to the cage. There was no time to go over
it or to go around it. He hurled himself straight
in and brought up with a shock against the wires
of the partition. At the same instant there was
a loud click behind him. The door snapped
down tight. And the weasel, unable to check
himself, bumped his nose against the wires with a
violence that brought the blood and stirred his
hunting lust to a madness of fury.

Both pursuer and pursued recovered themselves
in a second. It was well that the boy, an exact,
methodical soul, had lashed the cage securely to
the trunk, otherwise the mad assaults of the weasel

would have torn it loose and dashed it to the ground. He was all over it and around it every moment, flinging himself viciously this way and that in the effort to catch his quarry against the wires. And the quaking squirrel at the same time dashed himself frantically from side to side, keeping ever as much space as possible between himself and those relentless blood-seeking jaws. He had not the wit or the coolness to crouch in the centre of the cage, where he might securely have chattered derision at his foe. He had not yet, perhaps, even arrived at the truth that his prison was his citadel, his tower of safety. But at length, as luck would have it, in one of his desperate bounds, he shot himself clean through the round opening into the second chamber, and, before he knew it, he was racing at a breathless pace in the vain effort to climb the wall of the spinning cylinder.

For a moment or two the weasel was non-plussed. He stopped short and stared at these amazing tactics of his victim, his thin lips wrinkled back from his pointed jaw and muzzle in a sort of soundless snarl. Then, apparently coming to the conclusion that such a farce had gone on long enough, he sprang with all his strength upon the top of the cylinder, in the direction in which it was spinning. It was a great mistake. The cylinder did not stop. It spun on and shot him off indignantly, head-first, into space, and brought him with a stupefying thud upon the roots of the nearest tree. Very sore and disconcerted, he picked himself up, gave one look at the spinning mystery, and slunk off behind the tree, in a humbleness of spirit such as few of his irrepressible tribe have ever known.

All but paralyzed by exhaustion and by the utter extremity of his fear, the flying-squirrel stopped racing with his wheel. With all four hand-like paws, and even with his teeth, he clung to the wires, till presently his weight brought it to a standstill. Then he crept through the exit and crouched, trembling and panting, on the floor of the outer chamber. Here, soon after sun-up, the boy, who was an early riser, found him. He was puzzled, was the boy, over that smear of blood on the cage door; but, finding no clew to the events of the night, he was obliged to lay the matter away among the many insoluble enigmas wherewith the ancient wood so continually and so mockingly provokes the invader of its intimacies.

THE THEFT

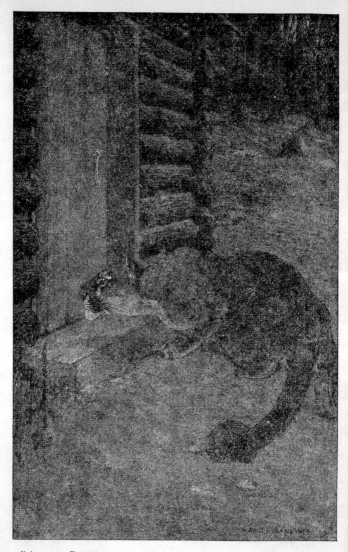

"At the Door-sill she listened long and intently, like a Cat at a Mouse-hole."

The Theft

FROM their cave in the cleft of Red Rock, where the half-uprooted pine-trees swung out across the ravine, the two panthers came padding noiselessly down the steep trail. In the abrupt descent their massive shoulders and haunches worked conspicuously under the tawny and supple hide, in a loose-jointed way that belied their enormous strength. Where the trail came out upon a patch of grassy level, starred with blossoms, beside the tumbling mountain stream, they parted company — the female turning off across the tangled and rocky slopes, while the male went on down to hunt in the heavy timber of the valley-bottom. Game was scarce that spring, and the hunt kept them both busy. They had no misgivings about leaving their two blind sprawling cubs to doze on their bed of dry grass in the dark inner corner of the cave. They knew very well that in all their range, for a radius of forty or fifty miles about the humped and massive hog-back of Red Rock, there was no beast so bold as to trespass on the panther's lair.

It was, perhaps, a half hour later that a man

came in sight, a half-breed squatter, moving stealthily up the farther bank of the stream. His dark figure appeared and disappeared, slipping from rock to tree, from tree to wild-vine thicket, as he picked his way furtively along the steep and obstructed slope. Not a twig cracked under his moccasined steps, so carefully did he go, though the soft roar of the stream would have covered any such light sound from all ears but the initiated and discriminating ones of the forest kindreds. His small watchful eyes took note of the grassy level on the other side of the stream, and, with a sure leap to a rock in mid channel, he came across. He arrived just a few feet below the spot where the female panther had taken her departure, digging in her broad pads heavily in the take-off of her leap. The grasses, trodden down in the heavy footprints, were still slowly lifting their heads. At sight of this trail, so startlingly fresh, the man crouched instantly back into the fringing bush, half lifting his rifle, and peering with vigilant eyes into the heart of every covert. He expected to see the beast's eyes palely glaring at him from some near ambush.

In a few minutes, however, he satisfied himself that the panther had gone on. Emerging from the bushes, he knelt down and examined the footprints minutely. Yes, the trail was older than he had at first imagined, by a good half hour. Some of the trodden grass had perfectly recovered itself, and a crushed brown beetle was already surrounded by ants. He arose with a grim smile, and traced the trail back across the grass-patch till it mingled with the confusion of footprints, going and coming, which led up the mountains. In this confusion he overlooked the traces of the other panther, so he was led to the conclusion that only one of the pair had gone out. If this was the path to the lair, as he inferred both from the number of the tracks and the fitness of the country, then he must expect to find one of the pair at home. His crafty and deep-set eyes flamed at the thought, for he was a great hunter and a dead shot with his heavy Winchester.

For days the half-breed had been searching for the trail and the den of the panther pair. His object was the cubs, who, as he knew, would be still tiny and manageable at this season. A good panther skin was well worth the effort of the chase, but a man in the settlements, who was collecting wild animals for a circus, had offered him one hundred and fifty dollars for a pair of healthy cubs. The half-breed's idea was to get the cubs as young as possible, and bring them up by bottle in his cabin till they should be big enough for delivery to the collector.

Before starting up the steep and difficult trail, the man examined his rifle. A panther at home, protecting her young, was not a foe with whom he could take risks. She commanded the tribute of his utmost precaution.

A careful survey of the slope before him convinced his practised eye that the den must be somewhere in that high cleft, where the broken faces of the red sandstone glowed brightly through dark patches and veils of clinging firs. He marked the great half-fallen pine-tree, with its top swung out from the rock face, and its branches curling upward. Somewhere not far from that, he concluded, would he come upon the object of his search.

Difficult as was the ascending trail, now slippery with wet moss, now obstructed with thick low branches which offered no obstacle to the panthers, but were seriously baffling to the man, he climbed swiftly and noiselessly. His lithe feet, in their flexible moose-hide moccasins, took firm hold of the irregularities of the trail, and he glided over or under the opposing branches with as little rustling as a black snake might have made. Every few moments he stiffened himself to the rigidity of a stump, and listened like a startled doe as he interrogated every rock and tree within reach of his eyes. Ready to match his trained senses against those of any of the wilderness kin, he felt confident of seeing or hearing any creature by which he might be seen or heard. Mounting thus warily, in some twenty minutes or there-abouts he came out upon a narrow shelf of rock beneath the downward swing of the old pine-tree.

Cautiously he peered about him, looking for some indication of the cave. This, as he told himself, was just the place for it. It could not be very far away. Then suddenly he shut himself down upon his heels, as if with a snap, and thrust upward the muzzle of his Winchester. Lifting his eyes, he had seen the black entrance of the cave almost on a level with the top of his head. A little chill ran down his spine as he realized that for those few seconds his scalp had perhaps been at the mercy of the occupant.

Why had the beast not struck?

The man took off his old cap, stuck it on the muzzle of his gun, and, raising it cautiously, wagged it from side to side. This move eliciting no demonstration from within the cave, he scratched noisily on the rock. Having repeated this challenge several times without response, he felt sure that both panthers must be away from home.

Nevertheless, he was not going to let himself be over-confident. He was too sagacious and instructed a woodsman to think that the wild creatures would always act the same way under the same circumstances. It was not impossible that the occupant of the cave was just waiting to see. Drawing back some six or eight feet, the man wriggled slantingly up the slope of rock, with the muzzle of his Winchester just ahead of him, till his face came level with the entrance. Every muscle of his body was strung taut for an instantaneous recoil, in case he should see before him two palely flaming eyes, afloat, as it were, upon the darkness of the interior.

But no; at first he could see nothing but the darkness itself. Then, as his eyes adapted themselves to the gloom, he made out the inmost recesses of the cave, and realized that, except for a vague little heap in one corner, the cave was empty. In that case, there was not a single moment to be lost. With one piercing backward glance down the trail, he slipped into the cave, snatched up the two kittens, regardless of their savage spitting and clawing, and thrust them into an empty potato-sack which he had brought with him for the purpose. Hurriedly twisting a cord about the neck of the sack, he wiped his bleeding hands upon his sleeve with a grin, slung the sack over his left shoulder, and hurried away. Having captured the prize, he was quite willing to avoid, if possible, any immediate reckoning with the old panthers.

Till he reached the grass-patch by the stream he took no pains to go silently, but made all possible haste, crashing through the branches and sending a shower of small stones clattering down the ravine. The angry and indomitable kittens in the bag on his back kept growling and spitting, and trying to dig their sharp claws into him, but his buckskin shirt was tough, and he paid no attention to their protest. At the edge of the torrent, however, he adopted new tactics. Leaping to the rock in mid channel, he crossed, and then, with great difficulty, clambered along close by the water's edge, well within the splash and the spray. When he had made a couple of hundred yards in this way, he came to a small tributary brook, up which he waded for some eighty or a hundred feet. Then, leaving the brook, he crept stealthily up the bank, through the underbrush, and so back to the valley he had just left, at a point some little distance farther downstream. Thence he ran straight on down the valley at a long easy trot, keeping always, as far as possible, under cover, and swerving from time to time this way or that in order to avoid treading on dry underbrush. His progress, however, was quite audible, for at this point in the venture he was sacrificing

secrecy to speed.   He had fifteen or sixteen miles
to go, his cabin being on the farther slope of the
great spur called Broken Ridge, and he knew that
he could not feel absolutely sure as to the out-
come of the enterprise until he should have the
little captives secure within his cabin.

As he threaded his way through the heavy
timber of the valley bottom, a good six or seven
miles from the den in Red Rock, he began to
feel more at ease.   Here among the great trunks
there was less undergrowth to obscure his view,
less danger of the panthers being able to steal up
upon him and take him unawares.   He slackened
his pace somewhat, drawing deep breaths into his
leathern lungs.   But he relaxed no precaution,
running noiselessly now over the soft carpet of
the forest, and flitting from tree-trunk to tree-
trunk as if an enemy were at his very heels.   At
last, quitting the valley, he started on a long
diagonal up the near slope of Broken Ridge
Spur.

The face of the country now suddenly changed.
Years before, a forest-fire had traversed this slope
of the ridge, cutting a clean swathe straight along
it.

The man's ascending trail thus led him across
a space of open, a space of undergrowth hardly
knee-deep, dotted with a few tall "rampikes," or

fire-stripped tree-trunks, bleached by the rains and inexpressibly desolate. Having here no cover, the man ran his best, and finally, having crossed the open, he dropped down in a dense thicket to rest, breathing hard from that last spurt.

In the secure concealment of the thicket he laid aside the complaining burden from his back, stood his rifle in a bush, let out his belt a couple of holes, and stooped to stretch himself on the moss for a quick rest. As he did so, he cast a prudent eye along his back trail. Instantly he stiffened, snatched up his gun again, sank on one knee, and insinuated the muzzle carefully between the screening branches. A huge panther had just shown himself, rising into view for an instant, and at once sinking back into the leafage.

At this disappearance the man grew uneasy. Was the beast still trailing him, belly to earth, through the low undergrowth? Or had it swerved aside to try and get ahead of him, to ambuscade him by and by from some rock or low-hung branch. Or, on the other hand, had it given up the pursuit rather than face the perils of the open? The man was annoyed at the uncertainty. Raising himself to his full height in order to command a better view of the trail, but at the same time keeping well hidden, he stood hesitating, doubtful whether to hurry on as fast as possible or to wait a while in this safe ambush in the hope of getting a shot at his pursuer.

*　　　*　　　*　　　*　　　*

Back to the cleft in Red Rock, beneath the down-swung pine, came the female panther. She had been lucky. She had made a quick kill, and satisfied her hunger, and now she was hurrying back to nurse her cubs.

Just before the door of the cave she caught the scent of the man. The fur arose angrily along her neck and backbone, and she entered in anxious haste. Instantly she came out again, whining and glancing this way and that as if bewildered. Then she plunged in again, sniffed at the place where the kittens had lain, sniffed at the spots where the man's feet had stepped, and darted out once more upon the ledge. But her appearance was very different now. Her eyes blazed, her long and powerful tail lashed furiously, and her fangs were bared to the gums in anguished rage. Lifting her head nigh, she gave vent to a long scream of summons, piercing and strident. The cry reached her mate, and brought him leaping in hot haste from his ambush beside a spring·pool where he was waiting for the appearance of some thirsty deer. But it did not reach the ears of the running man, who was at that moment threading a dense coppice far down the valley. Having sent out her call across the wide silence, she waited for no response, but darted down the trail. The tracks of the despoiler were plain to follow, and her nose told her that they were a good half hour old. She followed them down to the water's edge, out on to the rock and across the torrent. Then she lost them.

When her mate arrived, crouching prudently behind a thick fir-bush, to reconnoitre before he sprang out into the grass, she was bounding frantically from one side of the stream to the other, her enormously thick tail upstretched stiffly, as a sort of rudder, through the course of each prodigious leap. For a moment or two the pair put their heads together, and the mother, apparently, succeeded in conveying the situation to her mate in some singularly laconic speech. Almost at once, as it seemed, their plans were completed. The two started downstream, one along each bank. A couple of minutes more, and the man's trail was picked up by the female. A low cry notified the male, and he instantly sprang across and joined her.

It seems probable, from the female's future actions, that the two bereaved animals had now a fairly right idea of what had happened. The absence of blood, or sign of disturbance in the den or on the trail, conveyed to them the impression that their little ones had been carried off alive, because, to a wild creature, death is naturally associated with blood. It is possible, moreover, that there was nothing so very strange to them in the fact that the man should wish to carry off their cubs alive. What was so precious to themselves might very well be precious to others also. Mother birds, and mother quadrupeds as well, have been known, not infrequently, to steal each other's young. If, then, the panthers imagined that their kidnapped little ones were still alive, the furious quest on which they now set forth had a double object — vengeance and rescue.

They ran one behind the other, the female leading, and they went as noiselessly as blown feathers, for all their bulk. From time to time, being but short-winded runners, and accustomed rather to brief and violent than to long-continued effort, they would pause for breath, sniffing at the trail as it grew rapidly fresher, and seeming to take counsel together. Their pursuit at length grew more stealthy, as they approached the further side of the timbered valley, and realized that their enemy could not now be very far ahead.

The two panthers knew all that it concerned them to know about the man, except his object in robbing them of their little ones. They had often watched him, followed him, studied him, when he little guessed their scrutiny. They knew where

he lived, in the cabin with one door and one window, at the back of the stumpy clearing on the
side of Broken Ridge. They knew his wife, the
straight, swarthy, hard-featured woman, who wore
always some bright scarlet thing around her neck
and on her head. They knew his black-and-white
cow, with the bell at her neck, which made sounds
they did not like. They knew his yoke of raw-
boned red steers, which ploughed among the
stumps for him in the spring, and hauled logs for
him, laboriously, in the winter. They knew the
disquieting brilliance which would shine from his
window or his open door in nights when all the forest was in darkness. Above all, they knew of his
incomprehensible power of killing at a distance,
viewlessly. On account of this terrible power, they
had tried to avoid giving him offence. They had
refrained from hunting his cow or his steers; they
had even respected his foolish, cackling chickens,
being resolved in no way to risk drawing down
his vengeance upon them. Now, however, it was
different.

As the two grim avengers followed the trail,
like fleeting shadows, a red doe stepped leisurely
into their path before she caught sight of them.
For one instant she stood like a stone, petrified
with terror. In the next, she had vanished over
the nearest bushes with such a leap as she had

never before achieved. The female might have sprung upon her neck almost without effort. But she never even raised a paw against this easy quarry; it was a higher hunting that now engrossed her.

When at length the two running beasts came to the edge of the open ground on the slopes of Broken Ridge, they hesitated. The female, though the more deadly in the persistence of her hate, was at the same time the more sagacious. First of all, she wanted to recover her cubs. No mere vengeance could be so important to her as that. She shrank back into deeper cover, and started off to one side to skirt the dangerous open. But noticing that her mate was not following her, she stopped and looked back at him inquiringly.

The male, more impetuous and more bent upon mere revenge, showed himself for a moment beyond the fringe of the woods. In that one moment, though it was impossible that he should have detected the man in his hiding across the open, he nevertheless seemed to receive some impression from the man's challenging eyes. He felt that his enemy was there, in that dense clump of young firs. Instantly he dropped upon his belly in the undergrowth, flattening himself to an amazingly inconspicuous figure. Then he began creeping, slowly and with infinite stealth, out across the space of peril, beneath the full, revealing glare of the sun.   The female gave vent to a low whimper, trying to call him back.   Failing in that, she stood and watched him anxiously.

She could just see his tawny back moving through the light green leafage of the scrub.   He was crawling more swiftly now.   He had covered nearly half the distance.   All at once there came a spurt of flame from the fir thicket, and a sharp cracking report.   In the next instant she saw her mate rise straight into the air on his hind legs, clawing savagely.   Then he seemed to fall together and tumble over backwards.

She knew very well what had happened.   This was the power of the man.   She knew her mate was dead.   A further sullen heat was added to her hate, but it did not make her reckless.   She ran away down the slope, skirted the open at a safe distance, and closed in once more upon the man's trail a good mile farther on.   She had got ahead of the fugitive, for even now she heard the faint thud-thud of his loping feet.   She hid herself far up a tree, some thirty feet from the trail, and waited.

As the man came up, she eyed him with a mingling of mad hatred and anxious question. She saw the bundle on his back writhe violently, and she caught a little growling complaint which came from it. That settled her policy. Had she thought that the cubs were dead, she might have dropped upon the man from her post of vantage. But the cubs were alive. For their sakes she would take no risks with the man.

When he had passed on, she followed at a safe distance. The strange procession crossed the ridge. It neared the clearing and the cabin. At this point the panther heard, some little way back from the trail, the tonk-tonk of a cow-bell. There was no need of following the man so very closely for the moment. She swerved aside, ran straight, like a cat going for milk, through the thickets, and, with a burst of intolerable fury, sprang upon the cow's neck. There was not even a struggle, for the animal's neck was broken before it had time to know what was happening. The desperate mother tore her victim, but ate none of it. Then she hurried on toward the cabin. At least she had tasted some beginnings of vengeance.

As she reached the edge of the clearing, and came in sight of the cabin, the man was just entering the door, with the precious bundle in his hands. She saw the door close behind him. At this she whimpered uneasily, and started around to skirt the clearing and come upon the cabin from the rear.

As she went, she caught sight of the two red steers, feeding in the pasture field close by the fence. She crept up, eying them, but too sagacious to reveal herself in the open. As luck would have it, one of the steers at this moment came up close to the fence, to scratch his hide on the knots. With a snarl the panther struck at him through the rails, and drew a long ragged gash down his flank. Snorting with pain and terror, the steer turned and raced for home, tail in air; and his comrade, taking the alarm, bellowed nervously and followed him.

A few minutes later the man came out of his cabin, followed by his wife. The steers were at the barn door — a place they usually avoided at this season. One of them was shivering and bleeding. The man examined the wound, and understood. Turning to the woman, he said, —

"That there's the *mother's* work. We must hunt her down an' settle her to-morrer, or she'll clean out the farm."

Letting the frightened steers into the barn, he waited anxiously for the *tonk-atonk* of the black-and-white cow coming home to be milked. When she did not come, that, too, he understood only too well, and his wide mouth set itself grimly. It looked as if those were going to be an expensive pair of cubs.

After dark, late, the mother stole close up to the cabin. Everything was shut up tight — barn, shed, and house alike. At the door-sill she listened long and intently, like a cat at a mouse-hole. Her fine ear made out the heavy breathings of the man and the woman within. It also at length distinguished some faint little growlings and gruntings, such as the cubs only uttered when they were well fed. She prowled around the house all night, the pale flame of her savage and anxious eyes glowing upon it from every direction. Then, at the edge of dawn, she stole away, but not far, to a hiding-place whence she could command a view of the cabin-door. It was within that door that her cubs had vanished.

The sun was not a half hour high when the man set forth, and the woman with him, to hunt down the dangerous adversary whom they had challenged. The woman, who carried a rifle of the same pattern as the man's, was almost as sure a shot as he. The continued absence of the cow, the wound on the red steer's flank, the defiant network of tracks all about the cabin, showed clearly enough that the fight was now to the death. The man and woman knew there would be no security for them as long as the mother panther remained alive. Therefore they were in haste to settle the matter. They picked out a distinct trail and followed it. It led them straight to the body of the slain cow, which the slayer had visited twice in the course of the night, just to satisfy her thirst for vengeance.

But at the moment when the two indignant hunters were examining the carcass of the cow, the panther was at their cabin-door, listening. She had seen the man and woman hurry away. Now she could hear quite distinctly the little complainings of her young. She pushed against the heavy door till it creaked, but there was no entrance for her by that way. Close by was the window. Standing up on her hind legs, she stared in. At last she managed to make out the two cubs, lying in a corner in a box of rags and straw. The sight scattered all her caution to the winds. Scrambling up to the window-sill, she dashed her head and shoulders through the glass. That the jagged fragments cut her mouth and muzzle severely, she never heeded at all. Forcing her whole body through, her powerful haunches caught the window-frame, and carried it with them to the floor. Writhing herself free of this encumbrance, she darted to the box of rags, snatched up one of the cubs by the loose skin of its neck, sprang through the window with it, and bore it off into a growth of tall rank grass behind the barn. Returning at once to the cabin, she rescued the other cub in the same way, and brought it triumphantly to its brother in the long grass.

About this time she heard the man and the woman coming back. Instead of trying to get away, she coiled herself flat in the grass and began to suckle the cubs to keep them quiet. Her hiding-place was the most secure that she could have found within miles of the cabin, the man having never any occasion to go behind the barn — as she had seen by the absence of tracks — and the rank growth furnishing a very complete concealment. Crafty woodsman though the man was held to be, it never entered his mind that so shy a beast as the panther would take covert thus within the very stronghold of the foe. At sight of the shattered window he fell into a rage, and when he found the cubs gone, he exhausted ingenuity in consigning to every torment the man who had tempted him into speculating in panther cubs. Storming noisily, he hunted everywhere, except behind the barn. For a time his wife sat composedly on the wood-pile, and cheered him with pointed backwoods sarcasms. At last, however, the two went away over the ridge, to recover the skin of the other panther before it should be spoiled by foxes. During their absence the mother got both cubs safely carried off to a hollow tree some five miles farther along the ridge. That

night, while the man and the woman slept, with
boards nailed over their window, she bore them
far away from the perilous neighborhood.   By
difficult paths, and across two turbulent streams,
she removed them into the recesses of the neighboring county, a barren and difficult region,
where the wanderings of the man were little
likely to lead him.

THE TUNNEL RUNNERS

The Tunnel Runners

THE deep copper-red channel of the little tidal river wound inland through the wide yellowish levels of the salt marsh. Along each side of the channel, between the waving fringes of the grass and the line of usual high tide, ran a margin of pale yellowish-brown sand-flats, baked and seamed with sun cracks, scurfed with wavy deposits of salt, and spotted with meagre tufts of sea-green samphire, goose-tongue, and sea-rosemary. Just at the edge of the grass-fringe an old post, weather-beaten and time-eaten, stood up a solitary sentinel over the waste, reminder of a time when this point of the river had been a little haven for fishing-boats — a haven long since filled up by the caprice of the inexorable silt.

Some forty or fifty paces straight back from the mouldering post, a low spur of upland, darkly wooded with spruce and fir, jutted out into the yellow-green sea of grass. Off to the left, some hundred yards or so away, ran a line of round-topped dike, with a few stiff mullein stalks fringing its crest. Beyond the dike, and long ago reclaimed by it from the sea, lay basking in the sun the vast expanses of sweet-grass meadow, blue-green with timothy, clover, and vetch, and hummed over by innumerable golden-belted bumblebees. Through this sweet meadow wound the slow curves of a placid and brimming fresh-water stream, joining itself at last to the parent river through an *abat-d'eaux* in the dike, whose sunken valves protected it completely from the fluctuation of the tides.

The dividing line between the tall, waving, yellow salt grass and the naked mud-flat was as sharp as if cut by a diker's spade, and it was fringed by a close brown tangle of grass-roots, which seemed to feel outward over the baked mud and then curl back upon themselves in apprehension. Close to the foot of the mouldering post, where this fringe half encircled it, appeared suddenly a pointed brownish head, with tiny ears and a pair of little, bright, bead-like eyes set very close together. The head was thrust cautiously forth from the mouth of a narrow tunnel under the grass-roots. The sharp, overhung muzzle, with nostrils dilating and quivering, interrogated the perilous outer air; the bead eyes searched the sky, the grass-fringe, the baking open of the flat. There was no danger in sight; but just in front, some five or six feet distant, a gaudy caterpillar on some bold venture bent was making his slow way across the scurfed mud, from one goose-tongue tuft to another.

The pointed head shot swiftly forth from the tunnel, followed by a ruddy-brown body — straight out across the bright naked space, and back again, like a darting shuttle, into the hole, and the too rashly adventuring caterpillar had disappeared.

A little way back from the edge of the flats a mottled brown marsh-hawk was flying hither and thither. His wings were shorter and broader than those of most members of his swift marauding race, and he flew flapping almost like a crow, instead of gliding, skimming, and soaring, after the manner of his more aristocratic kindred. He flew close above the swaying grass-tops, his head thrust downward, and his hard, unwinking eyes peered fiercely down between the ranked coarse stems of the "broad-leaf" grass. He quartered the meadow section by section, closely and methodically as a well-handled setter. Once he dropped straight downward into the grass abruptly, as if he had been shot; and when, an instant later, he arose again, with a great buffeting of the grass-tops, he was clutching some tiny gray object in his talons. Had one been near enough to see, it would have proved, probably, to be a young shrew. Whatever it was, it was too small to be worth carrying off to his high perch on the

dead pine-tree beyond the ridge of the uplands.
He flew with it to the open crest of the dike
close by, where he devoured it in savage gulps.
Then, having wiped his beak on the hard sod, he
dropped off the dike and resumed his assiduous
quartering of the salt grass.

About this time the little brown, pointed head
with the bead eyes reappeared in the mouth of
the tunnel by the foot of the post. Everything
seemed safe. The samphire and the goose-tongue
tufts, palely glimmering in the sun, were full of
salt-loving, heat-loving insects. Warily the
ruddy-brown body behind the pointed head
slipped forth from the tunnel, and darted to the
nearest tuft, where it began nosing sharply and
snapping up small game.

The marsh-mouse was a sturdy figure, about
six inches in length, with a dull chestnut-brown
back sprinkled with black hairs shading downwards
through warm gray to a delicate fawn-colored
belly. Its shoulders and short forelegs were
heavily moulded, showing the digger of tunnels,
and its forepaws moved with the swift precise
facility of hands. The tiny ears were set flat
and tight to the head, and the broad-based skull
over the triangular muzzle gave an impression of
pugnacious courage, very unlike that of the wood-
mouse or the house-mouse. This expression was

more than justified by the fact, for the marsh-mouse, confident in his punishing little jaws and distrustful of his agility, had a dangerous propensity to stay and fight when he ought to be running away. It was a propensity which, owing to the abundance of his enemies, would have led speedily to the extermination of his race but for the amazing and unremitting fecundity which dwelt in his blood.

For all his courage, however, there were some foes which he had no inclination to meet and face —even he, one of the biggest and strongest of his kind. As he glanced aside from his nosing in the samphire tufts, he caught sight of a broad black splotch of shadow sweeping up the baked surface of the flat at terrific speed.

He did not look up; he had no need to. Only too well he knew what was casting that sinister shadow. Though agility was not supposed to be his strong point, his movement, as he shot across the open from the samphire tuft to the mouth of his tunnel, was almost too quick to follow. He gained the root-fringed door just in time. As his frantic, cringing hind quarters disappeared into the hole, the great talons of the pouncing hawk plunged into the root-fringe, closing and clutching so savagely that the mouth of the tunnel was obliterated. Grass-roots, however, were not what those rending talons wanted, and the great hawk, rising angrily, flapped off to the other side of the dike.

Within the tunnel the brown mouse ran on desperately, as if he felt those fatal talons still reaching after him. The tunnel was not quite in darkness, for here and there a gleam of light came filtering through the roots which formed its roof, and here and there a round opening gave access to the yellow-green world among the big stiff grass-stalks. The floor was smooth from the feet and teeth of countless other marsh-mice, water-voles, and marsh-shrews. To right and left went branching off innumerable side-tunnels and galleries, an apparently inextricable maze. But the brown mouse raced straight on, back from the waterside, deep into the heart of the marsh, anxious only to put himself as far as possible from the scene of his horrid adventure.

Running thus suddenly, he bumped hard into a little wayfarer who was journeying in the opposite direction. The tunnel was so narrow that only by the use of a certain circumspection and consideration could two travellers pass each other comfortably. Now the stranger was a mole-shrew, much smaller than the brown mouse, but of a temper as unpleasant as that of a mad buffalo. That the mouse should come butting into him in

that rude fashion was an indignity not to be tol-
erated. Gnashing his long, chisel-like teeth, he
grappled blindly, and rent the brown mouse's ear
to ribbons. But this was a mistake on his part,
a distinct error of judgment. The brown mouse
was no slim timorous barn-mouse or field-mouse,
no slow and clumsy mole. He was a fighter and
with strength to back his pugnacity. He caught
the angry shrew by the neck, bit him mercilessly,
shook him limp, trod him under foot, and raced
on. Not until he reached his snug nest in the
burrow at the foot of the dike did he quite regain
his equanimity.

Just about this time there came a succession of
heavy southwest gales, which piled up the water
into the funnel-like head of the bay, dammed back
the rivers, and brought a series of high tides.
Tides as high were quite unseasonable, and caught
the swarming little tunnel runners of the salt
marsh unprepared. As the first flood came lap-
ping up over the sun-baked flats, covering the
samphire tufts, setting all awash the root-fringes
of the grass, and sliding noiselessly into the tunnels,
there was a wild scurrying, and a faint elusive
clamor of squeaks came murmuring thinly up
through the grass. Myriads of brown-and-orange
grasshoppers, beetles black and green and blue
and red, with here and there a sleek grub, here

and there a furry caterpillar, began to climb the long, stiff grass-stalks. The battalions of the mice and voles and shrews, popping up indignantly through the skylight of the tunnels, swept unanimously toward the barrier of the dike. Every one of them knew quite well that to the sweet meadows beyond the dike the peril of the tide could not pursue them.

The big brown marsh-mouse, as it chanced, was asleep at the bottom of his burrow. Stealing up between the grass-stems, a chill douche slipped in upon him. Startled and choking, he darted up the steep slope of his gallery, and out into the wet turmoil. He was an expert swimmer, but he liked to choose his own time for the exercise of his skill. This was not one of the times. For one second he sat up upon his sturdy little haunches, squeaking angrily and surveying the excitement. Then, shaking his fur free of the few drops of water which clung to it in tiny globules, he joined the scurrying migrant throngs which were swarming through the dike.

Along the dike-top the migrants were running the gantlet with death. With the first invasion of the tide across the flats, all the marsh-hawks of the neighborhood — some four or five — had gathered to the hunt, knowing well just what the flood would do for them. Also many crows had come. At intervals along the crest of the dike stood the hawks, with wings half spread, screaming excitedly, clutching at their victims and devouring them with unlordly haste. Two, already gorged, were flapping away heavily toward the forest-clad inland ridges, carrying limp trophies in their talons. As for the crows, there were perhaps two score of them, all cawing noisily, flying low along the crest of the dike, and alighting from time to time to stab savagely with their dagger-like beaks.

The big brown marsh-mouse, wise with experience and many escapes, took this all in as he mounted the slope of the dike. Marking a hawk just above him, he doubled nimbly back, jumping over half a dozen blindly blundering fugitives. Some ten feet farther along he again ascended. As he came over the crest, in a mob of shrews and smaller mice, he saw a glossy crow just dropping upon him. The eyes of the crow, impish and malevolent, were fixed, not upon him, but upon a small shrew close at his side. Imagining himself, however, the object of attack, the brown mouse fell into a rage. Darting upward, he fixed his long teeth in the black marauder's thigh, just above the leg joint, and pulled him down into the scurrying stream of rodents. With a squeak of rage and alarm, the crow struck out savagely.

His murderous beak stabbed this way and that in the crowd, laying out more than one soft-bodied victim, while his strong black wings beat others into confusion and panic. But in the throng swarming over the dike at that point were many more of the marsh-mice and the shrews, all savage in temper. They leaped upon the crow, ran over and bore down the buffeting wings, and tore vengefully at the hard iridescent armor of close-laid feathers which shielded their foe from any fatal wounds. In spite of this disadvantage, they were wearing him out by sheer fury and weight of numbers, when the other crows came darkly to his assistance. In a moment he was liberated, and the dike-top strewn with gashed furry bodies. Bleeding and bedraggled, his eyes blazing with wrath, he sprang into the air and flapped away to the uplands to recover his composure in the seclusion of some dense pine-top. The brown marsh-mouse, the cause of his discomfiture, darted out from under his wing as he arose, and slipped over the edge of the dike with no worse injury than a red gash across the haunches. Having scored such a triumph over so redoubtable an enemy as the crow, he was not troubled by his wound; but discretion led him to plunge instantly into the deep green shelter of the grass.

Here in the sweet meadow, where the timothy

and clover stood much closer than did the coarse stalks of the "broad-leaf" in the salt meadow, the runways of the mice were not, as a rule, underground. They were made by gnawing off the stems close to the firm surface of the sod. The stems on each side, tending to be pressed together, formed a perfect roof to the narrow tunnels, which pierced the grass in every direction and formed a seemingly insoluble labyrinth. The brown mouse, however, knew his way very well through the soft green light, flecked with specks and streaks of pollen-dusty sunshine. The tunnels were swarming with travellers; but beyond nipping them on the haunches now and then, to make them get out of his way or move faster, he paid no attention to them. At last he came to the edge of the stream, and to a burrow beneath the roots of a wild-rose thicket which fringed the water.

This burrow the brown mouse had once inhabited. He felt it was his. Just now it was occupied by an irritable little mole-shrew; but the brown mouse, strong in the sense of ownership, proceeded to take possession. The outraged shrew put up a bitter fight, but in vain. With squeaks and blood the eviction was accomplished, and the brown mouse established himself complacently in the burrow.

After a few days the southwest gales blew themselves out, the tides drew back within their ordinary summer bounds, and most of the refugees returned to their old haunts among the "broad-leaf." But the brown mouse elected to remain in his burrow beside the rose-thicket. His taste had turned to the clover and timothy stalks, and the meadow was alive with brown crickets and toothsome, big, green grasshoppers. Moreover, in the heat of late July, he loved to swim in the bland waters of the stream, keeping close along shore, under the shadow of the long grass and the overhanging roses, and avoiding the dense patches of weed which might give shelter to the darting pickerel. His burrow was roomy and gave accommodation to a silken-furred brown mate, who set herself without delay to the duty of replenishing the diminished population of the marsh-mice.

In spite of foraging hawks, foxes, weasels, and minks, in spite of calamities, swift and frequent, overtaking this, that, and another of the innumerable kindred of the mice, the summer hours passed benignly over the burrow by the rose-thicket. Then, one sultry scented morning, there came a change. The deep quiet of the meadow went to pieces in blatant clamor. Loud-voiced men and snorting, trampling, clanking horses came to the edge of the grass, and with them two strange scarlet machines which clattered as they moved.

One of these scarlet monsters, dragged by its horses, swerved off toward the farther side of the meadow. The other started straight down through the deep grass along the edge of the stream. Into the grass, belly-deep, the big horses plunged, breasting it like the sea. Instantly the scarlet machine, which was ridden by a man, set up a new cry. It was a harsh, strident, terrifying cry, as if a million twanging locusts had found one voice. Before it, to the amazed horror of all the furry, scurrying grass-dwellers, the grass went down flat in long ranks. The peril of the floods was as nothing to this loud uncomprehended peril. Marsh-mice, water-voles, shrews, with here and there a foraging musk-rat, here and there a murderous and ravaging weasel, all fled frantically before it. A few, a very few, fled too late. These never knew what happened to them, for great darting knives, dancing unseen through the grass close to the earth, caught them and slew them.

The high cry of the deadly scarlet thing, however, gave warning fair and sufficient. As the big brown marsh-mouse heard it approaching, he dived straight to the bottom of his burrow and lay there trembling. His companion, on the other hand, holding different views as to the proper place of safety, darted from the burrow, wriggled through the thorny stems of the rose-thicket, and plunged into the water, where she hid herself close under the opposite bank. The noise and the darting knives glided almost over the mouth of the burrow, and the thumping heart of the brown mouse almost burst itself with terror. But they passed. Slowly they marched away. And when they had grown comparatively faint, far down at the foot of the meadow, beside the dike, the brown mouse, recovering himself, dared to peep forth. He was astonished to see a long breadth of grass lying prostrate, with bewildered bumblebees and grasshoppers striving to extricate themselves from the ruins. Having a valiant heart and a quick eye for opportunity, he sprang out of his hole and began pouncing on the confused and helpless insects. This, for a few minutes, was a profitable game, and a safe one, too, for the strident noise, with the presence of the men and horses, had driven hawks and crows to a discreet distance. But presently the cry of the scarlet thing, which had turned at the dike and was moving straight up the middle of the meadow, began to grow loud again, and the brown mouse whisked back into his burrow.

All through the time of the haying the meadow-folk lived in a turmoil of alarm and change. At first, under the heavy prostrate ranks of the slain grass, they ran bewildered but secure, for their foes could not easily detect them. For another day they were comparatively safe under the long scented lines of the dying "windrows," full of grasshoppers and wilted clover-heads. When the windrows were tossed together into innumerable pointed hay-cocks, they crowded beneath the ephemeral shelter, to be rudely bared next day to the blinding sun as the cocks were pitched into the rumbling hay-carts. It was a day of horrors, this, to the meadow kindreds, for a yellow Irish terrier, following the hay-makers, would run with wild yelpings under the lifted cocks, and slay the little people by the hundred. But as for the brown mouse, all this time he and his temporary mate dwelt secure, keeping to their burrow and to the barren but safe tunnels which they had driven amid the roots of the rose-thicket.

When the hay was gone — part of it carted away to upland barns, part built cunningly into high conical stacks — the meadow-dwellers found that they had fallen on evil times. The naked meadow, all bare close stubble, open to the eyes of hawk and crow by day, and of the still more deadly owl by night, had become their worst foe.

Some drew back to the fringes of the uplands. Some colonized along the winding edges of the stream. Some returned across the dike to the salt meadow, where the broad-leaf grass was not yet ripe for mowing; while the remnant huddled precariously under the bases of the stacks, an easy prey for every foraging weasel. In a little while, however, the short thick herbage of the aftermath thrust its head above the stubble. Then new tunnels were run, and life for the scurrying and squeaking meadow-folk once more began to offer its normal attractions. It was now more perilously insecure, however, for the herds of cattle turned to pasture on the aftermath kept it eaten down; and the shrewd crows learned that their beaks could pierce the fragile and too-open roofs of the tunnels.

At last the snow came, the deep snow and the hard cold, enemy to almost all the other kindred of the wild, but friendly to the mouse-folk. The snow, some two feet deep all over the meadows, over the dikes, and to the eating edges of the tides, gave them a perfect shelter, and was exactly suited to the driving of their tunnels. Food was abundant, because they could subsist very well on the nutritious root-stalks of the grass. And none of their enemies could get at them except when they chose to seek the upper air. In the daytime they kept to the glimmering blue light of the tunnels, but at night they would slip forth and play about the firm surface of the snow. It was then that they suffered, for though the hawks were gone, and the crows asleep, the icy winter night was alive with owls; and foxes, weasels, and minks would come prowling hungrily down from the uplands. The owls were the worst peril by far — marsh-owls, barn-owls, the darting little Acadian owls, swift as the sparrow-hawk; and now and then the terror of the winter wilds, the giant snowy owl of the North, driven down by storm and famine from his bleak Arctic wastes. The revels of the mouse-folk over their dim-lit playgrounds were varied with incessant tragedy. But the memories of the little people, fortunately, were short. Their perilous diversions went on unchecked, while their furry battalions thinned amazingly.

But through all these dangers the brown marsh-mouse went his way secure. He kept every exit of his tunnels perfectly hidden among the thorny tips of the wild rose-bushes, which stood up some five or six inches above the top of the snow. The successive families which were born and grew up in his safe burrow passed out into the maze, to be merged in the precarious and passing legions. His first mate disappeared mysteriously, and as

he had no facilities for pressing an inquiry among
the hawks or weasels, he never knew the details
of her disappearance. Her place was speedily
filled in the burrow. But to the brown mouse
himself nothing happened. He confined his
nightly revels beneath the moon to the region
of the rose-thickets, and so eluded effectually the
eyes and claws of the owls.

It was along toward the end of winter, however,
when the brown mouse met with his most dangerous adventure. Shunning, as he did so craftily, the games on the open snow, he was wont to
amuse himself — and incidentally seek variations
in his diet — beneath the ice of his threshold
stream. An expert swimmer and diver, almost
as swift as his cousin the musk-rat or his heredi-
tary enemy the mink, he would swim long dis-
tances under the water, finding fresh bits of
lily-root, tiny clams, water-snails, half-torpid
beetles, and many kinds of larvæ. As the
stream had been high at the time of freezing,
and had afterwards shrunken in its channel, letting the ice down with it, there were many air-
chambers along the brink, between ice-roof and
water surface; and slanting downward to the
nearest of these he had dug himself a tunnel
from the roots of his thicket. Even here, to be
sure, there were perils for him. There was one

big mink which loved to hunt along these secret and dim-lit air-chambers, taking long swims beneath the ice. But he was an autocrat, and kept all rival minks away from his range; so the wise brown mouse knew that as long as he kept a sharp enough lookout against that foe, he was secure in the air-chambers. Then, in the stream itself, there was always the peril of the great pike, which had its lair at the bottom of the deep pool down by the *abat-d'eaux*. The brown mouse had seen him but once — a long, straight, gray-green, shadowy shape in the distance — but that one sight gave him counsels of caution. He never forgot, when in the water, to keep watch for that great darting shadow.

One day, when the brown mouse had swum far downstream, and was hurrying back home, he was alarmed by loud sounds on the surface of the ice, a little below his back door. Some one with an axe was chopping a hole in the ice. The brown mouse swam away downstream again as fast as he could, and the jarring noise of the axe-strokes, carried by the ice and by the water, seemed to follow him with terrifying concussions. Hiding himself in a remote air-chamber, he waited for the noises to cease. Then, with mingled trepidation and caution, he swam upstream again.

As he neared home, he saw a round beam of

light pouring downward to the stream's bed through a hole in the ice. In the midst of this light there hung, moving softly to the slow current, a big lump of fat pork. The brown mouse did not know it was pork, but he knew at once it was something very good to eat. Very cautiously he swam up to investigate it. There seemed to be no reason why he should not nibble it. In fact, he was just going to nibble it, when, just a few feet farther upstream, those terrifying sounds began again. The brown mouse took them as a warning, and fled back downstream in a panic.

In a few minutes the noise stopped, and the courage of the brown mouse returned. As he swam once more homeward, firmly resolved that he would taste that delectable mystery on his way, a chill in his spine made him remember the great pike, and look back.

There *was* the great pike, a long dreadful shadow, gliding up behind him.

The brown mouse, as we have said, was a wonderful swimmer. He swam now as he had never swum before — a brown streak cleaving the dim-lit current; and as he went tiny water-bubbles, formed by the air pressed out from under his fur, flew up till they broke against the ice. But, with all his speed, the great pike swam faster, and was slowly overtaking him. Just as he passed that

strange dangling lump of pork, he realized that
this was a race which he could not win. The
entrance to his burrow was still too distant. But
he remembered a tiny air-chamber under the bank
close by. It had no exit. It was so small that
he might not find room there to haul himself
clear out of the water, beyond reach of his enemy's
jaws, but he had no choice, and in frantic suffocat-
ing desperation he dashed for it.

Even as he turned, however, the sense of doom
descended upon him. Was he not already too
late? The long awful shape of the great fish
was close upon him. With a convulsive effort
that almost burst his heart, he gained the air-
chamber, scrambled half-way out of the water, and
then, in that cramped space, turned at bay, game
to the last gasp.

To his amazement, the great pike was not at
his tail. Instead, he was still some three or four
feet away, out there just in the descending beam
of light from the hole in the ice. The mysterious
lump of pork had disappeared, but the gasping
brown mouse did not notice that. His attention
was engrossed in the amazing and terrifying per-
formances of the pike. The long gray-green
body was darting this way and that, in and out of
the beam of light, but never any great space out
of it. The great jaws shook savagely from side

to side, and then the mouse saw that from between them a slender gleaming cord extended upward through the hole. A moment more, and the pike sprang straight up, with a heavy swirl of the water, and vanished above the ice.

It was incomprehensible; and there was something altogether appalling about it. The brown mouse shivered. For several minutes he crouched there quite still, more utterly panic-stricken than he had ever been before in all his precarious little life. At last, with hesitation, he worked his way up along the bank, beneath the ice, to his own tunnel, and scurried in all haste to hide himself in the deepest corner of his burrow. And never thereafter could he comprehend why nothing more was seen, or heard, or rumored of the great pike.

A TORPEDO IN FEATHERS

"THE LOON AROSE COMPLETELY, AND SENT A LONG DERISIVE
PEAL OF HIS WILD LAUGHTER ECHOING DOWN THE LAKE."

A Torpedo in Feathers

THE blue kingfisher, flying over the still surface of the lake, and peering downward curiously as he flew, saw into its depths as if they had been clear glass. What he hoped to see was some small fish — chub, or shiner, or yellow perch, or trout, basking incautiously near the surface. What he saw was a sinister dark shape, elongated but massive, darting in a straight line through the transparent amber, some three or four feet below the surface. Knowing well enough what that meant — no fish so foolish as to linger in such dread neighborhood — the kingfisher flew on indignantly, with a loud clattering laugh like a rattle. He would do his fishing, according to his usual custom, in the shallower waters along shore, where the great black loon was less at home.

Darting straight ahead for an amazing distance, like a well-aimed torpedo, the loon came to a point where the lake-bottom slanted upward swiftly toward a bushy islet, over a floor of yellow sand that glowed in the sun. Here he just failed to transfix, with his powerful dagger of a bill, a big lake trout that hung, lazily waving its scarlet fins, beside a rock. The trout's golden-rimmed eyes detected the peril in time — just in time — and with a desperate screw-like thrust of his powerful tail, he shot aside and plunged into the shadowy deeps. The heavy swirl of his going disturbed an eight-inch chub, which chanced at the moment to be groping for larvæ in a muddy pocket beneath the rock. Incautiously it sailed forth to see what was happening. Before it had time to see anything, fate struck it. Caught in the vice of two iron mandibles, it was carried quivering to the surface.

All power of escape crushed out of it by that saw-toothed grip, the victim might safely have been dropped and devoured at leisure. But the great loon was too hungry for leisure. Moreover, he was an expert and he took no risks. With a jerk he threw the fish into the air, caught it as it fell head first, and gulped it down. For a moment or two he floated motionless, his small, fierce and peculiarly piercing eyes warily scrutinizing the lake in all directions. Then, lifting his black head, which gleamed in the sun with green, purple, and sapphire iridescence, he gave vent to a strange wild cry like a peal of bitter laughter. The cry echoed hollowly from the desolate shores of the lake. A moment or two later it was answered, in the same hollow and disconcerting tones, and from behind the islet his mate came swimming to meet him.

For a few minutes the two great birds swam slowly around each other, uttering several times their weird cry. As they floated at their ease, un-alarmed, they sat high in the water, showing some-thing of the clean pearly whiteness of their breasts and under parts. Their sturdy, trimly modelled bodies were about three feet in length, from the tips of their straight and formidable green beaks to the ends of their short stiff tails. Their heads, as we have seen, were of an intense and iridescent black, their necks encircled by collars of black and white, their backs, shoulders, and wings dull black, with white spots and bars. Their feet, very large, broadly webbed, and set extraordinarily far back, almost like those of a penguin, glimmered black as they fanned back and forth in the clear amber water.

Suddenly some movement among the bushes along the near shore, perhaps two hundred yards away, caught their watchful eyes. In an instant, by some mysterious process, they had sunk their bodies completely below the surface, leaving only their snaky heads and necks exposed to view. This peculiar submerged position they held, it seemed, without difficulty. But whatever it was that alarmed them, it was not repeated; and after perhaps five minutes of cautious watchfulness, they slowly emerged and floated on the surface. Presently the female swam back again behind the islet, laboriously scrambled out upon the shore, waddled to her nest, and settled herself once more to the task of brooding her two big gray-green, brown-blotched eggs. It was the first week in June, and the eggs were near hatching.

The pair of loons were restless and annoyed. Their lake, set in a lonely valley, which was drained by a branch of the Upper Quah-Davic, had seemed to them the perfection of solitude and remoteness. For three years now they had been coming to it every spring with the first of the northern flight. But this spring their solitude had been invaded. A pioneer, a squatter, with a buxom wife and several noisy children, had come and built a cabin on the shore of the lake. To be sure, the lake was large enough to overlook and forget such a small invasion, but for the loons it was a great matter. That cabin, those voices, and laughter, and axe-strokes, and sometimes gun-shots, though almost a mile away from their nesting-place, were a detestable and unpardonable intrusion.

The loon was just about to resume his fishing — a business which, on account of his phenomenal appetite, took up most of his time — when once more a movement in the bushes caught his vigilant eye. At the same instant a flash of white fire jetted through the leafy screen, a vicious report rang out, and a shower of shot cut the water into spurting streaks all about him. But he was not there. Inconceivably swift, he had dived at the flash itself. The lead that would have riddled him struck the empty swirl where he had vanished. A lanky youth with a gun stepped out from behind the bushes, stared in sulky disappointment, and presently strolled off down the shore to look for less elusive game.

The shattered calm of the lake surface had time to rebuild itself before the loon reappeared. A hundred yards away from the spot where he had dived, his head thrust itself above the water, a tiny black speck on the silvery sheen. It disappeared again instantly. When it once more came to the surface, it was so far out from shore that its owner felt safe. After a few moments devoted to inspection of the hunter's retreating form, the loon arose completely and sent a long derisive peal of his wild laughter echoing down the lake. The lanky youth turned and shook his fist at him, as if threatening to settle the score at a later day.

The loon had come by this time to a part of the lake where the depth was not more than six or seven feet, and the bottom was of rich firm mud, covered with rank growths. Here and there a solitary lily-plant, a stray from the creamy-blossomed, nectar-breathing colony over in the near-by cove, lifted to the surface its long pipe-like stems and flat sliding disks of leaves. It was a favorite resort, this, of almost every kind of fish that inhabited the lake, except, of course, of the minnows and other little fry, who would have been promptly made to serve as food for their bigger kinsmen had they ventured into so fatal a neighborhood.

Floating tranquilly, the loon caught sight of the silvery sides of a fat chub, balancing just above the bottom, beside one of the slender pipes of lily-stalk. The fish was lazily opening and closing its crimson gills, indifferent and with a well-fed air. It hung at a depth of perhaps six feet, and at a distance of perhaps sixteen or twenty. So smoothly as scarcely to leave a swirl on the surface, the loon dived straight down, then darted for the fish at a terrific pace. His powerful feet, folding up and opening out at each lightning-swift stroke, propelled him like a torpedo just shot from tube, and tiny bubbles, formed by the air caught under his feathers, flicked upward along his course.

The chub caught sight of this shape of doom

rushing upon him through the golden tremor of the water. He shot off in a panic, seeking some deep crevice or some weed-thicket dense enough to hide him. But the loon was almost at his tail. There was no crevice to be found, and the weed thickets were too sparse and open to conceal him. This way and that he darted, doubling and twisting frantically around every stalk or stone. But in spite of his bulk, the loon followed each turn with the agility of an eel. The loosed silt boiled up in wreaths behind his violent passage, and the weeds swayed in the wake of the thrusting webs. In less than a minute the chase — the turmoil of which drove every other fish, large or small, in terror from the feeding-ground — came suddenly to an end. Rising abruptly with the fish gripped in his great beak, the loon burst out upon the surface, sending shoreward a succession of circling ripples. Without ceremony he gulped his meal. Then, swimming rather low in the water, and with head thrust out before him, he hurried to his nesting-place on the islet, as if he thought he had been too long away from his domestic duties.

The spot on the islet where the loons had their nest was almost unconcealed. It was in a grassy cup within four or five feet of the water's edge, and sheltered only by a thin screen of bushes on the landward side. Tow-

ard the sky it was quite open. There had
seemed to be little need of concealment before the intruder, man, came to the lake. The
islet was too far from the main shore to be in
danger from the visits of foxes or bears, fishers
or raccoons. And as for the sky — well, the
loon had little fear of anything that flew. Because of this lack of apprehension from skyward, even his coloring was not very pro-
tective, his glossy black, barred and mottled
with pure white, being fairly conspicuous
against the grays, and greens, and browns
which surrounded the nest. Neither he nor
his mate had any particular objection to being
seen by any marauder of the air. Even the
murderous goshawk, or the smaller but even
more fearless duck-hawk, would know better
than to swoop down upon the uplifted dagger
of a nesting loon. And as for the eagle,
though doubtless strong enough to master
such an antagonist in the end, he is wise
enough to know that the loon's punishing
beak and bulldog courage in defence of the
nest would make the victory an expensive
and painful one.

But there was one enemy besides man
whom the loons had cause to fear, even on
their secluded islet. They hated the mink

with a well-founded hate. He could easily swim out to discover and rob their nest; and if he should find it for a moment unguarded, his agility would enable him to keep well clear of their avenging wrath. On the nest neither male nor female feared to meet the mink's attack, their lithe necks and unerring quickness of thrust being sufficient defence even against so formidable a robber. But their movements on land — an awkward, flopping series of waddles — were so slow that, in the case of a mink arriving, the precious eggs would be safe only while actually covered. A big mink had been seen that very morning, prowling down the opposite shore, and both birds were uneasy. They seemed now to be taking counsel upon that or some other equally important matter.

For the next few days, however, the life of the loons was tranquil, with good fishing to content their appetites and no untoward event to make them anxious. Then came a day when the patient mother on her nest could not conceal her happiness and her excitement, when the male, forgetful of meals, stood for hours at a time in interested expectancy beside the nest. The strong chicks within the eggs were beginning to stir and

M

chip the shell. It was not the day that the big mink should have chosen for his expedition to the islet.

For several weeks the mink had been on the point of swimming out to explore that little patch of rocks and grass and bushes, sentinelled by one dark fir-tree. Such a secluded spot, out of reach of most forest prowlers, might well afford something special in the way of good hunting. Hitherto one thing or another had always diverted him from his purpose, and he had gone off on another trail. But to-day nothing intervened. His long, lithe, black body curving like a snake's, he ran down the bank, lifted his triangular vicious-looking head for a survey of the lake, and plunged into the water with a low splash.

Now, the vision of the mink, though sharp enough at close quarters, has nothing like the power and penetration of the loon's. The mink could see the islet, the rocks, the bushes, the sentinel fir-tree, but he could not make out the figure of the loon standing beside the nest. The loon, on the other hand, could see him with absolute distinctness, as if not more than fifty feet away.

As has been already noted, the day was not well chosen for the mink's trip to the islet. The loon stiffened himself with anger, and his round bright eyes hardened implacably. The mother settled down closer over the stirring eggs, and turned her head to stare malevolently at the long pointed trail which the swimmer's head was drawing on the lake surface. Her mate stood for some seconds as motionless as a charred stump. Then, slipping noiselessly down the bank, he glided into the water and dived from sight.

The lake was deep at this point, the main channel of the stream — upon which the lake was threaded like a great oval bead on a slender string — running between the islet and the mainland. The loon plunged nearly to the bottom, that he might run no risk of being detected by the enemy. More than ever like a torpedo, as he pierced the brown depths, he darted forward to the attack. Two or three great lake trout, seeing the approach of the black rushing shape, made way in terror and hid in the deepest weed-patch they could find. But the loon was not thinking of fish. The most tempting tit-bit in the lake at that moment might have brushed against his feathers with impunity.

At last, still far ahead of him, he saw the enemy's approach. As he looked upward through the water, the under surface was like a radiant but half transparent mirror, on which the tiniest floating object, even a fly or a wild-cherry petal, stood

out with amazing distinctness. The dark body
of the swimming mink was large and black and
menacing against its setting of silver, and the
ripples spread away from his chin, ever widening,
till they faded on the shore behind him. The
loon kept straight on till the mink was almost
above him, then he turned and shot upward.

Thinking, doubtless, of some wild duck's nest,
well filled with large green eggs, which he would
devour at his ease after sucking the blood of the
brooding mother, the mink swam on steadily toward the islet. The worn gray rocks and fringing
grass grew nearer, and the details began to sepa-
rate themselves to his fierce little eyes. Presently
he made out the black shape of the female loon
sitting on her nest and eying him. That prom-
ised something interesting. The blood leaped
in his veins, and he raced forward at redoubled
speed, for the mink goes into his frays with a
rampant blood-lust that makes him always formidable, even to creatures of twice his weight.

It was just at this moment that his alert senses
took note of a strange vague heaving in the water
beneath him, a sort of dull and broad vibration.
Swiftly he ducked his head, to see if the whole
lake-bottom was rising up at him. But he had
no time to see anything. It was as if a red-hot
iron was jabbed straight upward through the

tender back part of his throat, and a swarm of stars exploded in his brain. Then he knew nothing more. The loon's steel-like bill had pierced to and penetrated the base of the skull, and with one convulsive kick, the robber's body straightened itself out upon the water. Shaking his head like an angry terrier, he wrenched his bill free and hurried back to reassure his mate, leaving the body of the mink to sink languidly to the bottom. Here, among the weeds, it was presently discovered by the eels and crawfish, faithful scavengers, who saw to it that there should be nothing left to pollute the sweet lake-waters.

On the following day the two awkward, dingy-hued, downy chicks were hatched, and thenceforth the parents were kept busy supplying their extremely healthy appetites. The havoc wrought among the finny hordes — the trout and "togue" [1] and chub, the red-fins, shiners, and minnows — was enormous. The loon chicks, enterprising and industrious, speedily learned to help their parents by hunting the small fry in the sunlit shallows along shore.

But the loon family were not the only ardent fishermen on those waters. The new-comers,

---

[1] The "togue" is a peculiar gray lake trout, of northern New Brunswick, which grows to a great size, and is caught with bait or a spoon.

the man family, they too liked fish, and had no
mean skill in catching them. In fact, their methods
were stupidly and slaughterously destructive, well
calculated to quite draw out the lake in two or
three seasons. They set a big purse-seine right
across the channel, and, worst of all, they dragged
the deep dark pools, wherein, now that the waters
were growing warmer under the mid-June sun,
the biggest trout and "togue" were wont to
gather for coolness. Their own thought was to
get their larder well stocked with salted fish
against the coming winter. Future winters might
look out for themselves.

For some time the great loon, though more
enterprising and wide-ranging than his prudent
mate, had kept careful distance from the nets
and net-stakes, as from all the other visible mani-
festations of man. But at last he grew accustomed
to the tall immovable stakes in the channel which
supported the purse-seine. He concluded that
they were harmless, or even impotent, and decided
to investigate them.

As he approached, the dim meshes of the net,
shimmering vaguely in the bright water, excited
his suspicions. He sheered off warily and swam
around the seine at a prudent distance. At last
he found the opening. There seemed to be no
danger anywhere in sight, so, after some hesitation,

he sailed in. The ordered curving rows of the stakes, the top line of the net, beaded with a few floats, here and there rising above the water — it was all very curious, but it did not seem in any way hostile. He eyed it scornfully. For what was neither dangerous nor useful he had a highly practical contempt. Having satisfied his curiosity, and allayed a certain uneasiness with which he had always regarded the great set-net, he turned to swim out again. But at this moment he chanced to look down.

The sight that met his eyes was one to stir the blood of any fisherman. He was just over the " purse " — that fatal chamber whence so few who enter it ever find the exit. The narrow space was crowded with every kind of fish that frequented the lake, except for the slim eels and the small fry who could swim through the meshes. It was the chance of a loon's lifetime. Flashing downward, he darted this way and that ecstatically among the frantic prisoners, transfixing half a dozen in succession, to make sure of them, before he seized a big trout for his immediate meal. Gripping the victim savagely in his bill, he slanted toward the surface, and plunged into a slack bight of the net.

Luckily for him, he was within a foot of the air before he struck the deceitful meshes. Carried on by the impetus of his rush, he bore the net upward with him, and emerged into the full sun. In the shock of his surprise he dropped the fish, and at the same time gulped his lungs full of fresh air. For perhaps half a minute, he thrust and flapped and tore furiously, expecting to break through the elusive obstacle, which yielded so freely that he could get no hold upon it, yet always thrust him back with a suave but inexorable persistence. At length, realizing himself foiled in this direction, he sank downward like a stone, thinking to back out of the struggle and rise somewhere else. But, to his horror, the bight of the net came down with him, refusing to be left. In his struggles he had completely enmeshed himself.

And now, probably for the very first time in a not uneventful life, the great loon lost his head. He began to fight blindly, overwhelmed by panic terror. Plunging, kicking, beating with half-fettered wings, striking with his beak in a semi-paralyzed fashion because he had not room to stretch his neck to its full length, he was soon utterly exhausted. Moreover, he was more than half drowned. At last, a dimness coming over the golden amber light, he gave up in despair. With a feeble despairing stroke of his webbed feet, he strove to get back to the surface. Happily for him, the net in this direction was not relentless.

It yielded without too much resistance, and the hopelessly entangled prisoner came to the top. Lying there in the meshes, he could at least draw breath.

When, a little later in the day, he saw a boat approaching up the lake with two of the dreaded man creatures in it, he gave one final mighty struggle, which lashed the water into foam and sent the imprisoned fish into fresh paroxysms; and then, with the stoicism which some of the wild creatures can display in the moment of supreme and hopeless peril, he lay quite still, eying the foe defiantly.

One of the beings in the boat was that lanky youth whose attempt to shoot the loon had been such a conspicuous failure. The other was the lanky youth's father, the pioneer himself. At the sight of the trussed-up captive, the youth shouted exultantly ——

"It's that durn loon what's eatin' all the fish in the lake! I'll fix his fishin'!" and, lifting his oar from the thole-pins, he raised it to strike the helpless bird.

"Don't be sich a *durn* fool, Zeb!" interrupted the father. "Ye'll get more money for that bird alive, down to Fredericton, than all the fish in the net's worth. A loon like that ain't common. He's a beauty!"

The youth dropped his oar and leaned over to snatch up the prize. But he jumped back with alacrity as his father snapped: "*Look out!*"

"What for?" he demanded, rather sheepishly.

"Why," replied the older man, "he'll stick you like a pig with that knife beak of his'n, if ye don't look sharp! Reach me yer jacket. We'll wrap up his head till we kin get him clear o' the net."

The youth obeyed. Helplessly swathed in the heavy homespun jacket, whose strong man smell enraged and daunted him, the great bird was disentangled from the net and lifted into the boat. Laughingly the father passed the bundle along the gunwale to his son.

But swathing a powerful bird in a jacket is a more or less inexact undertaking, as many have found in experimenting with wounded hawks and eagles. By some lucky wriggle the loon got his head free. Instantly, with all the force of his powerful neck-muscles, he drove his beak half-way through the fleshy part of his old enemy's arm. With a startled yell the lad dropped him. He bounded from the gunwale and rolled into the water. The man snatched at him and caught a flopping sleeve of the jacket. The jacket promptly and neatly unrolled, and the loon, diving deep, was out of sight in an eye-wink, leaving his would-be jailers to express themselves according to their mood. When he came to the surface for breath, he was a hundred yards away, and on the other side of the boat, and as he thrust little more than his beak and nostrils above water, he was not detected.

A few minutes more, and he was laughing derisively from the other side of the islet, swimming in safety with his mate and his two energetic chicks. Nevertheless, for all his triumph and the discomfiture of his foes, the grim experience had put him out of conceit with the lake. That same night, when the white moon rode high over the jagged spruce ridges, a hollow globe of enchantment, he led his little family straight up the river, mile after mile, till they reached another lake. It was a small lake, shut in by brooding hills, with iron shores, and few fish in its inhospitable waters, but it was remote from man and his works. So here the outraged bird was content to establish himself till the hour should return for migrants to fly south.

HOW A CAT PLAYED ROBINSON CRUSOE

How a Cat Played Robinson Crusoe

THE island was a mere sandbank off the low flat coast. Not a tree broke its bleak levels, not even a shrub. But the long, sparse, gritty stalks of the marsh-grass clothed it everywhere above tide-mark, and a tiny rivulet of sweet water, flowing from a spring at its centre, drew a riband of inland herbage and tenderer green across the harsh and sombre yellow-gray of the grass. One would not have chosen the island as an alluring place to set one's habitation, yet at its seaward end, where the changing tides were never still, stood a spacious, one-storied, wide-verandahed cottage, with a low shed behind it. The one virtue that this lone plot of sea-rejected sand could boast was coolness. When the neighbor mainland would be sweltering, day and night alike, under a breathless heat, out here on the island there was always a cool wind blowing. Therefore a wise city dweller had appropriated the sea waif, and built his summer home thereon, where the tonic airs might bring back the rose to the pale cheeks of his children.

The family came to the island toward the end of June. In the first week of September they went away, leaving every door and window of house and shed securely shuttered, bolted or barred, against the winter's storms. A roomy boat, rowed by two fishermen, carried them across the half mile of racing tides that separated them from the mainland. The elders of the household were not sorry to get back to the distractions of the world of men, after two months of the companionship of wind and sun and waves and waving grass-tops. But the children went with tear-stained faces. They were leaving behind them their household pet, the invariable comrade of their migrations, a handsome moon-faced cat, striped like a tiger. The animal had disappeared two days before, vanishing mysteriously from the naked face of the island. The only reasonable explanation seemed to be that she had been snapped up by a passing eagle.

The cat, meanwhile, was fast prisoner at the other end of the island, hidden beneath a broken barrel and some hundredweight of drifted sand.

The old barrel, with the staves battered out on one side in some past encounter with the tides, had stood half buried on the crest of a

sand-ridge raised by the long prevailing wind.
Under its lee the cat had found a sheltered
hollow, full of sun, where she had been wont to
lie curled up for hours at a time, basking and
sleeping.   Meanwhile, the sand had been steadily
piling itself higher and higher behind the un-
stable barrier.   At last, it had piled too high,
and suddenly, before a stronger gust, the barrel
had come toppling over beneath a mass of sand
burying the sleeping cat out of sight and light;
but at the same time the sound half of the barrel
had formed a safe roof to her prison, and she
was neither crushed nor smothered.   When the
children, in their anxious search all over the
island, came upon the mound of fine white sand,
they gave it but one careless look.   They could
not hear the faint cries that came at intervals
from the close darkness within.   So they went
away sorrowfully, little dreaming that their friend
was imprisoned almost beneath their feet.

For three days the prisoner kept up her inter-
mittent appeals for help.   On the third day the
wind changed, and presently blew up a gale.   In
a few hours it had uncovered the barrel.   At one
corner a tiny spot of light appeared.   Eagerly
the cat stuck her paw through the hole.   When
she withdrew it again, the hole was considerably
enlarged.   She took the hint, and fell to scratch-

N

ing. At first her efforts were rather aimless; but presently, whether by good luck or quick sagacity, she learned to make her scratching more effective. The opening rapidly enlarged, and she squeezed her way out.

The wind was tearing madly across the island, filled with flying sand. The seas hurled themselves trampling up the beach, with the uproar of a bombardment. The scourged grasses lay pallid, bowed flat in long quivering ranks. Over the turmoil the sun stared down from a deep unclouded blue. The cat, when she first met the full force of the gale, was fairly blown off her feet. As soon as she could recover herself, she crouched low and darted into the grass for shelter. But there was little shelter there, the long stalks being held down almost level as if by an implacable hand. Through their lashed lines, however, she sped straight before the gale, making for the cottage at the other end of the island, where she would find, as she fondly imagined, not only food and shelter, but loving comfort to make her forget her terrors.

Unutterably still and desolate in the bright sunshine, and under the howling of the wind, the house frightened her. She could not understand the tight-closed shutters, the blind unresponding doors that would no longer open to her anxious appeal. The wind swept her savagely across the naked veranda. Climbing with difficulty to the dining-room window-sill, where so often she had been let in, she clung there a few moments and yowled heart-brokenly. Then, in a sudden panic, she jumped down and ran to the shed. That, too, was closed. She had never seen the shed doors closed, and could not understand it. Cautiously she crept around the foundations, but those had been honestly and efficiently constructed. There was no such thing as getting in that way. On every side it was nothing but a dead face, dead and forbidding, that the old familiar house confronted her with.

The cat had always been so coddled and pampered by the children that she had had no need to forage for herself; but, fortunately for her now, she had learned to hunt the marsh-mice and grass-sparrows for amusement. So now, being ravenous from her long fast under the sand, she slunk mournfully away from the deserted house, and crept along, under the lee of a sand-ridge, to a little grassy hollow which she knew. Here the gale caught only the tops of the grasses, bending but not prostrating them; and here in the warmth and comparative calm, the furry little marsh-folk, mice and shrews, were going about their business undisturbed. The cat, quick and stealthy, soon caught one, and eased the ferocity of her hunger. She caught several. And then, making her way back to the house, she spent hours in heart-sick prowling, around it and around, sniffing and peering, yowling piteously on threshold and window-sill, and every now and then being blown ignominiously across the smooth naked expanse of the veranda floor. At last, hopelessly discouraged, she curled herself up out of the wind, beneath the children's window, and went to sleep.

On the following day the gale died down, and the salt-grass once more lifted its tops, full of flitting birds and small brown-and-yellow autumn butterflies, under the golden September sun. Desolate though the island was, it swarmed, nevertheless, with the minute busy life of the grass-stems and the sand-flats. Mice, crickets, sand-hoppers — the cat had no need to go hungry or unoccupied. She went all over house and shed again, from foundation to roof and chimney-top, yowling from time to time in a great hollow, melancholy voice that might have been heard all across the island had there been any one to hear, and again, from time to time, meowing in small piteous tones no bigger than a kitten's. For hours at a time when hunger did not drive her to the hunt, she would sit expectant on the window-ledge, or before the door, or on the veranda steps, hoping that at any instant door or window might

open, and dear familiar voices call her in. When
she did go hunting, she hunted with peculiar
ferocity, as if to avenge herself for some great but
dimly apprehended wrong.

In spite of her loneliness and grief, the life of
the island prisoner during the next two or three
weeks was by no means one of hardship. Besides
her abundant food of birds and mice, she quickly
learned to catch tiny fish in the mouth of the rivulet, where salt water and fresh water met. It was
an exciting game, and she became expert at dashing
the gray tour-cod and blue-and-silver sand-lance
far up the slope with a sweep of her armed paw.
But when the equinoctial storms roared down upon
the island, with furious rain and low black clouds
torn to shreds, then life became more difficult for
her. Game all took to cover, where it was hard
to find — vanishing mysteriously. It was hard
to get around in the drenched and lashing grass,
and, moreover, she loathed wet. Most of the
time she went hungry, sitting sullen and desolate
under the lee of the house, glaring out defiantly
at the rush and battling tumult of the waves.

The storm lasted nearly ten days before it blew
itself clean out. On the eighth day the abandoned
wreck of a small Nova Scotia schooner drove
ashore, battered out of all likeness to a ship. But,
hulk as it was, it had passengers of a sort. A

horde of bedraggled rats got through the surf and
scurried into the hiding of the grass-roots. They
promptly made themselves at home, burrowing
under the grass and beneath old half-buried
timbers, and carrying panic into the ranks of the
mice and shrews. When the storm was over, the
cat had a decided surprise in her first long hunting expedition. Something had rustled the grass
heavily, and she trailed it, expecting a particularly
large fat marsh-mouse. When she pounced and
alighted upon an immense old ship's rat, many-
voyaged and many-battled, she got badly bitten.
Such an experience had never before fallen to her
lot. At first she felt so injured that she was on the
point of backing out and running away. Then
her latent pugnacity awoke, and the fire of far-off
ancestors. She flung herself into the fight with a
rage that took no accounting of the wounds she got,
and the struggle was soon over. Hungry though
she was, she dragged the slain rat all the way to
the house, and laid it proudly on the veranda
floor before the door, as if displaying it to the
eyes of her vanished friends. For a few moments
she stood over it, waiting hopefully. Perhaps
she had a wistful idea that so splendid an offering
might melt the hearts of the absent ones and per-
suade them to come back. Nothing happened,
however, so she sadly dragged the prize down the

steps again to her accustomed lair in the sand, and ate it up all but the tail.   Her wounds, faithfully licked, soon healed themselves in that clean and tonic air, and after that, having learned how to handle such big game, she no more got bitten.

During the first full moon after her abandonment, the first week in October, the island was visited by still weather, with sharp night frosts. The cat discovered then that it was most exciting to hunt by night and do her sleeping in the daytime.   It was a natural reversion to the instincts of her ancestors, but it came to her as a discovery. She found that now, under the strange whiteness of the moon, all her game was astir, except the birds.   And the birds had all fled to the mainland during the storm, gathering for the southward flight.   The blanched grasses, she found, were now everywhere a-rustle, and everywhere vague, spectral, little shapes went darting, with thin squeaks, across the ghostly white sands. Also, she made the aquaintance of a new bird, which she regarded at first uneasily, and then with vengeful wrath.   This was the brown marsh-owl, which came over from the mainland to do some autumn mouse-hunting.   There were two pairs of these big, downy-winged, round-eyed, voracious hunters, and they did not know there was a cat on the island.

The cat, spying one of them as it swooped soundlessly hither and thither over the silvered grass-tops, crouched with flattened ears. With its wide spread of wing it looked bigger than herself, and the great round face, with hooked beak and wild staring eyes, appeared extremely formidable. However, she was no coward, and presently, though not without reasonable caution, she went about her hunting. Suddenly the owl caught a partial glimpse of her in the grass, probably of her ears or head. He swooped, and at the same instant she sprang upward to meet the assault, spitting and growling harshly, and striking with unsheathed claws. With a frantic flapping of his great wings, the owl checked himself and drew back into the air, just escaping the clutch of those indignant claws. But after that the marsh-owls were careful to give her a wide berth. They realized that the black-striped animal, with the quick spring and the clutching claws, was not to be interfered with. They perceived that she was some relation of that dangerous prowler, the lynx. But if they were disturbed by the presence on the island of so dangerous a rival as the cat, they were amply compensated by the coming of the rats, who afforded them fine hunting of a kind which they had never before experienced. In spite of all this hunting, however, the furry life of the marsh-grass was so teeming, so inexhaustible, that the depredations of cat, rats, and owls were powerless to make more than a passing impression upon it. So the hunting and the merrymaking went on side by side under the indifferent moon, and the untouched swarms whom Fate passed by were as indifferent as the moon herself to the mysterious disappearances of their fellows.

As winter drew on, with bursts of sharp cold and changing winds that forced her to be continually changing her refuge, the cat grew more and more unhappy. She felt her homelessness keenly. Nowhere on the whole island could she find a nook where she might feel secure from both wind and rain. As for the old barrel, the first cause of her misfortunes, there was no help in that. The winds had long ago turned it completely over, open to the sky, then drifted it full of sand and reburied it. And in any case the cat would have been afraid to go near it again; she had no short memory. So it came about that she alone, of all the island dwellers, had no shelter to turn to when the real winter arrived, with snows that smothered the grass-tops out of sight, and frosts that lined the shore with grinding ice-cakes. The rats had their holes under the buried fragments of wreckage; the mice and shrews had their deep warm tunnels; the owls had nests in

hollow trees far away in the forests of the mainland. But the cat, shivering and frightened,
could do nothing but crouch against the blind
walls of the unrelenting house, and let the snow
whirl itself and pile itself about her.

And now, in her misery, she found her food
cut off. The mice ran secure in their hidden runways, where the grass-roots on either side of them
gave them easy and abundant provender. The
rats, too, were out of sight, digging burrows themselves in the soft snow, in the hope of intercepting
some of the tunnels of the mice, and now and
then snapping up an unwary passer-by. The ice-
fringe, crumbling and heaving under the ruthless
tide, put an end to her fishing. She would have
tried to capture one of the formidable owls, in her
hunger, but the owls no longer came to the island.
They would return, no doubt, later in the season,
when the snow had hardened, and the mice had
begun to come out and play on the surface, but
for the present they were following an easier chase
in the deeps of the upland forest.

When the snow had stopped falling, and the
sun came out again, there fell such keen cold as
the cat had never felt before. Starving as she
was, she could not sleep, but kept ceaselessly on
the prowl. This was fortunate for her, for had
she gone to sleep, without any more shelter than

the side of the house, she would never have
wakened again.   In her restlessness she wandered
to the farther side of the island, where, in a somewhat sheltered and sunny recess of the shore, fac-
ing the mainland, she found a patch of bare sand,
free of ice-cakes and just uncovered by the tide.
Opening upon this recess were the tiny entrances
to several of the mouse-tunnels.

Close beside one of these holes, in the snow, the
cat crouched, quiveringly intent.   For ten minutes or more she waited, never so much as twitching a whisker.   At last a mouse thrust out its
little pointed head.   Not daring to give it time
to change its mind or take alarm, she pounced.
The mouse, glimpsing the doom ere it fell,
doubled back upon itself in the narrow runway.
Hardly realizing what she did, in her desperation
the cat plunged head and shoulders into the snow,
reaching blindly after the vanished prize.   By
great good luck she clutched it and held it.

It was her first meal in four bitter days.

Now she had learned a lesson.   Naturally
clever, and her wits sharpened by her fierce necessities, she had grasped the idea that it was possible to follow her prey a little way into the snow.
She had not realized that the snow was so pene-
trable.   She had quite obliterated the door of
this particular runway, but she went on and

crouched beside another. Here she had to wait a long time before an adventurous mouse came to peer out. But this time she showed that she had grasped her lesson effectively. It was straight at the side of the entrance that she pounced, where instinct told her that the body of the mouse would be. One outstretched paw thus cut off the quarry's retreat. Her tactics were completely successful, and as her head went plunging into the fluffy whiteness, she felt the prize between her paws.

Her hunger now fairly appeased, she found herself immensely excited over this new fashion of hunting. Often before had she waited at mouse-holes, but never had she found it possible to break down the walls and invade the holes themselves. It was a thrilling idea. As she crept toward another hole, a mouse scurried swiftly up the sand and darted into it. The cat, too late to catch him before he disappeared, tried to follow him. Scratching clumsily but hopefully, she succeeded in penetrating the full length of her body into the snow. Of course she found no sign of the fugitive, which was by this time racing in safety down some dim transverse tunnel. Her eyes, mouth, whiskers, and fur full of the powdery white particles, she backed out, much disappointed. But in that moment she had realized that it was

much warmer in there beneath the snow than out
in the stinging air. It was a second and vitally
important lesson. And though she was probably
unconscious of having learned it, she instinctively
put the new lore into practice a little while later.
Having succeeded in catching yet another mouse,
for which her appetite made no immediate demand, she carried it back to the house and laid
it down in tribute on the veranda steps, while
she meowed and stared hopefully at the desolate
snow-draped door. Getting no response, she
carried the dead mouse down with her to the hollow behind the drift, which had been caused by
the bulging front of the bay-window on the end of
the house. Here she curled herself up forlornly,
thinking to have a wink of sleep.

But the still cold was too searching. She
looked at the sloping wall of snow beside
her, and cautiously thrust her paw into it.
It was very soft and light; it seemed to
offer practically no resistance. She pawed away
in an awkward fashion till she had scooped out
a sort of tiny cave. Gently she pushed herself into it, pressing back the snow on every
side, till she had room to turn around. Then
turn around she did several times, as so many
dogs do in getting their beds arranged to their
liking. In this process she not only packed

down the snow beneath her, but she rounded out for herself a snug chamber with a comparatively narrow doorway. From this snowy retreat she gazed forth with a solemn air of possession, then went to sleep with a sense of comfort, of " homeyness," such as she had never before felt since the disappearance of her friends.

Having thus conquered her environment, and won herself the freedom of the winter wild, her life, though strenuous, was no longer one of any terrible hardship. With patience at the mouseholes, she could catch enough to eat, and in her snowy den she slept warm and secure. In a little while, when a crust had formed over the surface, the mice took to coming out at night and holding revels on the snow. Then the owls, too, came back, and the cat, having tried to catch one, got sharply bitten and clawed before she realized the propriety of letting it go. After this experience she decided that owls, on the whole, were meant to be let alone. But, for all that, she found it fine hunting out there on the bleak, unfenced, white reaches of the snow.

Thus mistress of the situation, she found the winter slipping by without further serious trials. Only once, toward the end of January, did Fate send her a bad quarter of an hour. On the heels of a peculiarly bitter cold snap, a huge white owl from the Arctic barrens came one night to the island. The cat, taking observations from the corner of the veranda, caught sight of him. One look was enough to assure her that this was a very different kind of visitor from the brown marsh-owls. She slipped inconspicuously down into her burrow, and until the great white owl went away some twenty-four hours later, she kept herself discreetly out of sight.

When spring came back to the island, with the nightly shrill chorus of fluting frogs in the shallow sedgy pools, and the young grass alive with nesting birds, the prisoner's life became almost luxurious in its easy abundance. But now she was once more homeless, since her snug den had vanished with the snow. This did not matter much to her now, however, for the weather grew warmer and more tranquil day by day, and, moreover, she herself, in being forced back upon long latent instincts, had learned the heedless vagrancy of the wild. Nevertheless, with all her capacity for learning and adapting herself, she had not forgotten anything. So when, one day in June, a crowded boat came over from the mainland, and children's voices, clamoring across the grass-tops, broke the desolate silence of the island, the cat heard, and sprang up out of her sleep on the veranda steps. For one second she stood listening intently. Then, almost as a dog would have done, and as few of her supercilious tribe ever condescend to do, she went racing across to the landing-place, to be snatched up into the arms of four happy children at once, and to have her fine fur ruffled to a state which it would cost her an hour's assiduous toilet to put in order.

LITTLE BULL OF THE BARRENS

"The Whole Herd moved off toward the Northeast."

Little Bull of the Barrens

THROUGH the thick drive of the snow-flakes — small, hard, bitter flakes, borne on the long wind of the terrible Coppermine barrens — the man and the beast stood staring at each other, motionless. In the beast's eyes was a heavy wonder, mixed with curiosity and dread. Never before had he seen any being like this erect slim shape, veiled and vague and dark in the whirling drift. He felt it to be dangerous, but he was loath to tear himself away from the scrutiny of it.

The man, on the other hand, had neither wonder, curiosity, nor dread in his gaze. He knew that the black and massive apparition before him was a musk-ox. His first impulse had been to snatch up his rifle and shoot, before the beast could fade off into the white confusion of the storm. But his practised eye had told him that the animal was an old bull. His necessity was not fierce enough to drive him to the eating of such flesh — tough and reeking to nausea with musk. He wanted a young cow whose meat would be tender and sweet as caribou. He was content to wait, knowing that the herd must be near, and would not leave these feeding-grounds unless frightened. At this season the black bull, there staring at him heavily through the drift, would not be solitary.

The man was a trapper, who was making his way down the river to the Hudson Bay Company's post at the mouth. Through failure of the caribou to come his way according to their custom, his supplies had run short, and he was seeking the post in good time before the pinch of hunger should fix itself upon him. But he had had bad luck. The failure of the caribou had hit others besides himself. The wolves had suffered by it. Perhaps, in their shrewd and savage spirits, they had blamed the man for the absence of their accustomed quarry. Some weeks before his start they had craftily picked off his dogs — a reasonable and satisfying retaliation. And now the man was hauling the sledge himself.

In a moment's lift of the storm, the man had noted a little valley, a depression in the vast wind-swept level of the barrens, lying but a couple of stone's-throws aside from the banks of the river which was his guide. He knew that there he would find a dense growth of the stunted firs which spring up wherever they can find shelter from the wind. There he knew he would find dry stuff in plenty for his fire. There he would take covert till the storm should go down and suffer him to trail the musk-ox herd. After eying the black bull steadily for some minutes, he softly turned away, and without haste made for the valley of the little firs, dragging the laden sledge behind him.

The black bull snorted thickly and took several steps forward. The strange figure fading silently away through the drift evidently feared him. A fleeing foe was surely to be followed. But that long dark shape crawling at the stranger's heels — *that* looked formidable and very mysterious. The beast stopped, shook his head, snorted again more loudly, and drew back those few paces which he had advanced. Perhaps it was just as well not to be too bold in interrogating the unknown. After a few moments of hesitation he wheeled aside, lifted his massive and shaggy head, sniffed the air, listened intently, and withdrew to rejoin the little herd, which was lying down and contentedly chewing the cud, all indifferent to the drive of the polar storm.

The black bull of the barrens, as he stood and eyed contemplatively the resting herd, showed small in stature but extraordinarily massive in build. A scant six feet in length from muzzle to root of tail, and not much over three feet high at the shoulder, he was modelled, nevertheless, on lines that for power a mammoth might have envied. His square frame was clothed with long blackish hair reaching almost to the fetlocks. His ponderous head, maned and shaggy, was armed with short crescent horns, keen-tipped and serviceable for battle. And he carried it swung low, muzzle in and front well forward, always ready for defence against the enemies of the herd.

The herd numbered some dozen or fifteen cows, armed and powerful like their mates, several younger bulls, and perhaps a dozen yearling or two-year-old calves. At one moment, as the fierce drift slackened, they would all be more or less visible — shrouded, dark forms with contemplative eyes, peacefully ruminating. A moment more and they would vanish, as the snow again closed down about them.

It was the old bull alone who seemed to be thoroughly on the alert. Hither and thither, with a certain slow vigilance, he moved through the herd. All at once he lifted his head sharply and questioned the air with dilating nostrils, while his eyes gleamed with anger and anxiety. The next instant he stamped his foot and gave a loud abrupt call, half bleat, half bellow.

Plainly it was a signal well understood. In a

second the whole herd was on its feet.   In another, with lightning precision, it had formed itself into a compact circle, using the watchful leader as the basic point of its formation.   The calves, butted unceremoniously into the centre, hustled one upon the other, with uplifted muzzles over each other's shoulders and mild eyes staring with startled fright. The outer rim of the circle became a fringe of sullen lowering foreheads, angry eyes and keen horns jutting formidably from snow-powdered manes of dark hair.

Not a member of the musk-ox herd, to the youngest calf, but knew very well against what enemy the old bull had so suddenly marshalled them into fighting phalanx.   For some moments, however — long, tense, vigilant moments — nothing appeared.   Then at last, through the driving flakes, they caught sight of several gaunt, leaping forms, gray and shadowy, which swept down upon them in silence out of the storm.

With terrible suddenness and speed they came, these leaping forms, as if they would hurl themselves blindly upon the massed herd.   But the line of lowered horns never flinched or wavered, and with a short snarl from their leader the wolves swerved, just in time to escape a savage thrust from the old bull.   They swerved, strung out into line, and went loping round the circle, their narrowed, greenish, merciless eyes glaring into the obstinate ones of the musk-oxen. Again and again they circled the rampart of horns, again and again they drew off and swept up furiously to the assault, hoping to find some weak point in the defences — some timorous young cow who would shrink and swerve at their assault and open a breach in the line. But there was no cow in that herd afflicted with any such suicidal folly. The snow-spotted, lowering line of heads waited un-shaken, and presently the wolves — there were seven of them — bunched together a few paces from the circle and seemed to consider. Two of them sat down upon their haunches with their tongues hanging out, and eyed the rampart of horned fronts evilly, while the others stood with their heads together, or prowled restlessly back and forth. They might, indeed, with the vast leaping power of their long legs and muscular haunches, have sprung clear over the line of defence, and gained in two seconds the helpless calves in the centre; but they knew what that would mean. The herd would turn in upon them in a blind, uncalculating fury and trample them underfoot. For the moment, therefore, they hung waver-ing in irresolution, looking for a sign from the leader of the pack.

In the meantime the man had found his valley

hollow and the shelter of the expected colony of dwarf firs. Here the snow lay soft and undrifted. In a recess of the fir-thicket he trod it down with his snowshoes, and made haste to build himself a little fire of dead sticks. Above his head, above the shrouded fir-tops, above the rim of the hollow, the storm drove by unabated; but the snowflakes that escaped from the tumult to filter down into this retreat were too light and fine and dry to interfere with the fire. In two or three minutes the flames were crackling up clear and free, with little spittings and fine hissings where the flakes fell at their thin edges.

Having collected a pile of dry sticks within easy reach, the man stretched a couple of stitched caribou hides on poles to form a sloping roof over his head, cooked himself a hasty stew of pemmican and biscuit, made a hearty meal, and squatted before the fire with his back against his sledge, to smoke and wait. He knew how to wait, like an Indian, when there was anything to be gained by it, and his heart, weary of pemmican, was set on fresh meat.

There was no sign of the storm breaking; there was no use hunting in the storm. There was nothing to fear, for it was now three weeks since he had seen sign of the wolves which had eaten his dogs, and he knew that they had ranged off on the trial of the vanished caribou. There was nothing to do. He was warm and filled, and free from care. Some hundred miles or so away there was a post and human companionship, to which he looked forward with unhurried content. In due time he would arrive there and find it, as always before, unchanged, like all else in that land of inevitable recurrence. Meanwhile — this afternoon, perhaps, or to-morrow — he would shoot a young musk-ox cow. He drew his furs well about him and dozed off to sleep, knowing that the moment the fire began to get dangerously low an unfailing instinct would bid him awake to tend it.

While he slept, the storm drove unrelenting over the place of his retreat, and kept heaping the thin dry snow in fringes and wreaths upon the shaggy, lowering fronts of the musk-ox phalanx. From time to time, a massive head would shake off the burden and emerge black and menacing. And always, with unwavering vigilance, the army of angry eyes and short sharp horns confronted the group of discontented wolves.

Now, as it chanced, the trapper was wrong in his assumption as to the wolves. The truth — which would have made a great difference in his calculations had he known it — was that they had been cautiously trailing him ever since he left his hut. But they knew something of man, those wolves, and they feared him. They were not yet quite mad with hunger, so they had not yet quite plucked up courage to reveal themselves to him, still less to commit themselves to an open attack. They dreaded his eye, they dreaded his sharp, authoritative voice. They dreaded the strange, menacing smell of him. They dreaded his mysterious power of striking invisibly from very far off. Had they had any choice, they would far rather have been running down the caribou than trailing this solitary trapper. But the craving belly is a hard master, and they had no choice but to hasten wherever it scourged them on. Moreover, they knew along the trail of the man there were liable to be pickings, for man, a fastidious feeder, never eats all he kills.

When at last the trail of the man had led them into that of the musk-oxen, the pack had been glad. So much the more, therefore, their disappointed rage, when they found the herd ready for their attack, and too strong, in point of numbers and experienced leadership, to be stampeded. Seeing the prey so near, with each moment of their discomfiture their hunger and their fury grew.

Suddenly, without visible sign or warning, it seemed to boil over all at once. The whole pack sprang together, swift as the snap of a whip, into a compact mass, and hurled itself straight upon the circle of lowered horns. The charge looked irresistible. It seemed that the most dauntless must cringe and shrink before it.

But the point attacked was a strong one in the array. It was held by the wise old bull. To either side of him the shaggy black heads breathed hard or snorted loudly, but not a horn wavered. And in the face of this steadfastness the attack was not driven home. In the very last fraction of a second the leader swerved; the pack swept swiftly aside, but it was very close. As the hind-most wolf went by, the old bull lunged forward, head and shoulders beyond the circle, with a savage twist of his short, polished horns. There was a startled yelp. He had just managed to catch his foe a rending prod in the thick of the haunch. The wolf never paused — he was under the iron discipline of the pack, — but as he ran he left a scarlet trail along the snow behind him.

To the slow amazement of the herd, their enemies now, in the next instant, had vanished through the thin whirl of the drift. Heavy heads, thrust far out from the phalanx, turned to stare after them. There was nothing to be seen but the endless, sheeted procession of the snow. There was nothing to be heard but the muffled rush of

the wind and their own snortings and tramplings.
For a long time, however, they kept their array
unbroken, fearing a trick on the part of their adversaries.   Then at last the old bull, after sniffing
the wind in all directions with uplifted muzzle,
stepped forth from the ranks.   Immediately the
circle dissolved.   There was a moment of whirling and grunting, of butting at stupid calves or
reorganizing the array, then, at a swift walk, the
whole herd moved off toward the northeast, where
they knew of a region of low huddled hills which
would give them the kind of shelter that they loved.

In the meantime the pack, maddened by failure
and ravenous from the view of food denied, had
resumed the trail of the man.   They were different
beings now from the wary skulkers who had been
following him from afar.   Silent and swift, their
eyes flaming coldly and their thin lips wrinkled
back from long white fangs, they swept over the
brink and down into the windless hollow of the
stunted firs.

The man, sleeping in his furs by the little fire,
had a bad dream.   With a struggle and a yell he
awoke from it, to find himself half erect, upon one
knee, battling frantically for his life.   One great
hairy form he had clutched by the throat with
both hands, as its fangs snapped within an inch of
his face, and its huge hot breath daunted him with

a sense that the end of things had come. With a
monstrous effort he hurled it off, but in the same
moment he was borne down from behind. It
seemed to him that a wave of furred, fighting
bodies, enormous and irresistible, went over him,
blotting out everything, even to the desire of life.
He was but half conscious of the fangs that sank
into his flesh, strangely without pain. He was
but half conscious of struggling — the mere instinctive struggle of his strong muscles, and already
condemned as futile by his aloof and scornful
spirit. Then nothing but a knot of great gray
wolves, tussling and snarling over something on
the snow.

*   *   *   *   *

After everything on the sledge had been torn
open and investigated, and scattered over the
blood-stained snow, the wolves drew off to a little
distance from the fire, which they hated and
dreaded. It was a victory which would make
that pack for the future tenfold more dangerous.
They had dared and vanquished man. But what
was one man and a little bag of dry pemmican to
such hunger as theirs? All at once, as if moved
simultaneously by one impulse, they gathered, sped
up out of the firs into the wind, and swept away
through the storm on the trail of the musk-ox herd.

The herd, though travelling fast, had not gone

far.   On a sudden, as if at a premonition of peril,
the old bull halted with a loud snort.   Neither
smell nor sound of his enemies had reached him,
but he took alarm, and gave the signal to form
phalanx for defence, at the same time galloping
around the flank of the herd to close up and
strengthen the rear.   The evolution was prompt
and swift.   But before it was quite accomplished,
up from the white obscurity of the storm, in silence, came the leaping wolves.

Straight into the gap in the rear of the herd
they hurled themselves, slashing on every side
with the aim of spreading a panic.   A young
bull, just in the act of whirling furiously to con-
front the attack, was caught full on the flank, and
went down coughing, his throat torn clean out.
A young cow, with one wolf snapping at her side,
but failing to gain a vital spot, and another on her
back, biting for her neck through the matted
mane, went mad with terror, and charged straight
in among the calves at the centre of the herd,
making a way for the whole pack.

In a second several of the calves, bawling frantically, were pulled down.   The wolves, mad with
blood and their late triumph over the man, were
in a riot of slaughter.   The herd was cleft and
rent asunder to the heart.   The victory seemed
overwhelming.

But there was one thing which the pack had *not* reckoned with — the indomitable pluck and generalship of the old bull. Blindly confident in their leader, the herd hung together stolidly, instead of disintegrating. The front ranks turned inward upon the bloody convulsion of the centre. At the same time the old bull, followed by a couple of raging cows in quest of their young calves, came plunging in behind the pack and fell upon its rear like battering rams. In a moment the flanks closed in behind them, and the completed circle, instead of flying to pieces, began ponderously to constrict.

As the wolves realized what was happening, the two hindermost whirled about, just in time to leap savagely at the old bull's neck, one on each side. But they had no room to act effectively, no chance to choose their hold. As he charged with head down and the full impetus of his bulk, their fangs gashed him to the shoulder, but slantingly, so that the wounds were not deep. In his rage he never felt them. The next moment his two assailants were borne down, gored and trampled, by the frantic cows, while he lurched onward into the hideous *mêlée* at the centre. A second more, and the churning, snorting mass became wedged almost solid. Snapping silently at whatever was in reach, the

wolves were overborne, trodden down with the
dead or dying calves. The leader of the pack,
with two of the more astute of his followers, succeeded in dragging himself forth upon the packed
shoulders of his adversaries, ran over the heaving
sea of backs, and raced away through the storm,
gored and streaming. Soon there was no sign
of a wolf anywhere to be seen. But still the
packed herd went on with its trampling and
churning, sullenly resolute to make an end of
the matter, till even the sturdy unwounded calves
were in danger of being downed, and the weaker
ones perished miserably. At last, in some way,
the old bull managed to make his orders understood. The milling slackened, the pressure relaxed. Ponderously he shouldered his way out,
and started off once more toward the northeast.
Instantly the herd followed, lumbering at his
heels. A few, badly wounded, limped and staggered in the rear, and three cows, their ves rolling
wildly, remained standing over certain shapeless
masses that lay trodden into the red snow. For
some minutes they stood there, mooing disconsolately; then, one after the other, they shook their
shaggy heads and galloped away in pursuit of the
herd, appalled at the solitude and the sight of so
much death.

THE TIGER OF THE SEA

The Tiger of the Sea

THROUGH the broad, indolent, green-purple swells, ruffled and crisped along their tops by a mild breeze, the cow-orca went wallowing contentedly, her calf swimming close at her side. From time to time it rubbed against her, as if apprehensive in face of the vast and perilous spaces of the ocean, and seeking covert behind her short powerful flipper. And from time to time, being one of the most devoted and assiduous of all the mothers of the wild, she would gather it caressingly to her side with that great flipper, or, whirling half around, touch it inquiringly with her enormous rounded snout.

She was a good nineteen or twenty feet in length, the great orca — or " killer whale," as she would have been dubbed by any sailor or fisherman who might have chanced to cast eyes upon her. She would have been recognized at once, from all the other members of her whale-and-porpoise tribe, by the immense dorsal fin, not far from five feet high, rising erect from the broad and massive black curve of her back, by the two conspicuous white streaks on her black flank, and by the sharply defined line of her cream-white belly as she rolled lazily on the slope of a swell. All these were danger signals, which the knowing would have taken care to heed.

Little cause for apprehension had the calf of the orca, as long as it kept near its mother. For this most swift and savage of all the cetaceans feared nothing that swam, except her giant cousin, the cachalot or sperm-whale. Though but twenty feet long, she would attack and kill, through the sheer ferocity of her fury, the great whalebone or "right" whale, of fully four times her length and many times her bulk. Man she might have feared, had she ever learned his power; but, being poor in blubber, her tribe had never tempted man to so difficult and perilous a hunting. There were sharks, to be sure, that might equal or surpass her in size, but none to even approach her in savagery, speed, or cunning. It was in care-free content, therefore, that she lazed onward through the bland, untroubled sea, heedless alike of the surf on the yellow cliffs to her right, and of the empty spaces of ocean to her left. Such attention as she could spare from the baby charms of her calf was given to searching the transparent deeps below her, where lurked the big squid and slug-gish, bottom-feeding fish on which she habitually preyed.

Suddenly, with no sound but a vast sucking gurgle as the waters closed above her, she dived. Far down in the obscurity she had caught sight of a pallid, sprawling form. It was an octopus, which had been so ill-advised as to leave its customary home among the rocks of the bottom and seek new feeding-grounds. Before it had time even to attempt escape, the great jaws of the "killer" engulfed it. For one moment its eight long tentacles writhed desperately, clutching at its captor's lips. Then they vanished, sucked in and swallowed at a gulp. Thereupon the orca sailed leisurely back to the sunlit surface, met on her way up by her anxious calf, which had not been quite quick enough to follow its mother's lightning descent. She had not been two minutes absent, and never for an instant out of sight, but the youngster's instinct warned it well that the mild blue element in which it dwelt was full of dangers.

The octopus, though a large one, had been but a mouthful for the great killer, a stimulus, merely, to her vast appetite. She journeyed now with a keener eye upon the depths. Presently the deep blue-green of the water began to change to a lighter, beryl hue, where a line of making reef came up to within some thirty feet of the surface, and caught the sun. Here, basking, lay a broad, flat, bat-like creature, with wing-fins a dozen feet

across, and a long whip-like tail. Its cold moveless eyes, staring upward, caught sight of the
killer's body, slowly cleaving the surface. With
an almost imperceptible movement of the black
wings, it slid from the reef and plunged for refuge
in the depths.

But the giant ray had not been quick or stealthy
enough to evade its enemy's eye. Again the orca
dived, this time without heed of silence, and so
swiftly that her broad flukes, rising straight into
the air, came down upon the water with a report
that resounded all the way in to shore. Her
descent was straight as a plummet. The ray,
seeing it, was seized with panic. It darted to one
side, and shot upward again, at a terrific pace, on
a magnificent sweeping curve. With the force of
that uprush it hurled its whole black, shuddering
bulk clear into the air, where it turned, and for
one instant hung flapping darkly, as if the very
madness of its terror had driven it to the conquest
of a new element. To the nervous calf it was a
prodigy of horror, blotting out the sun. But
this violent excursion into the air was of only a
second or two's duration, and futile as it was
brief. As the flat black wings came down again,
with an enormous splash, the pursuing orca arose
almost beneath them, seized them, and dragged
them under. There was no fight, the ray being

powerless against its mighty adversary — only a moment's blind, frantic struggle in the foaming swirls, and then a spreading stain of red on the green sea.

This, now, was a fully sufficing meal, even for such an appetite as the orca's; and many neglected fragments of it went spreading and sinking away to feed the innumerable scavenging crabs that lurked in the weeds and hollows of the sunken reef. The orca, for the next half hour or so, remained where she was, rolling contentedly in the bright water above the reef, nursing and caressing her calf, and digesting her meal. Then she slowly continued her journey, but slanting in toward shore till she was not more than half a mile from the chain of precipitous islets and broken promontories which fringed this dangerous coast.

It was now full noon, and the unclouded sunlight, striking almost straight downward upon the surface of the sea, revealed the bottom at an amazing depth. Poised about half-way down the glimmering transparency, a large squid, or cuttle-fish, was swimming at leisure. His narrow, tapering body was about six feet in length, and perhaps twelve or fourteen inches in diameter at the broadest part, which was the head. From this formless head, seeming to sprout from it as leaf-stalks from a carrot, grew a bunch of tentacles, ten in number, and of about the same length as the body. Body and tentacles alike were of a pallid, dirty yellow-gray, with brownish spots — a color that made its wearer almost invisible in that sun-penetrated sea. The progress of the squid was backward; and he achieved it, not by moving his tentacles, but by sucking a volume of water into a great muscular sac beneath the tentacles and forcibly expelling it again. It looked as if he were breathing water and using it to blow himself along.

The orca was by no means hungry so soon after the feast which she had made on the giant ray, but the succulent morsel of the squid was a temptation not to be resisted. Tipping smoothly, her huge but finely modelled black-and-white form shot straight downward through the shimmering flood. But before she could reach him, the squid looked up and saw her. On the instant his ten loose tentacles tightened to a rigid bundle which offered no obstruction to his progress; his pale sides contracted with a mighty convulsion, expelling a volume of water which shot him along with the speed of a torpedo from its tube; and at the same time, from a gland within the propulsion sac, he squirted forth a jet of inky fluid which spread at once into a great cloud of black, veiling his flight. Behind that concealment he changed his direction, and fled downward toward a deep crevice in the rocky bottom, where he knew that the jaws of his enemy would not be able to reach him.

The orca, undeterred, plunged straight onward into the inky cloud. But once well within that gloom she lost all track of her intended prey. She also, for the moment, lost herself. This way and that she darted, snapping her vast jaws ravenously, but in vain. They closed on nothing but the empty and tainted water. At last, and quite unexpectedly, she emerged from the blackness into the transparent green, and, glancing upward, saw a sight which caused her to hurl herself madly to the surface with a Titanic sweep of her great flanks. That furious stroke made the depths boil like the thrust of a liner's propellers.

The calf, having started to follow its mother into the depths, had been frightened by that inky cloud into which it had seen her vanish. Returning in a flurry to the surface, it was swimming around aimlessly and anxiously, when it caught the eye of a wandering shark.

The shark, knowing very well what it was, looked around for the mother. He had no desire to be uncivil to a mother orca; but there was no mother in sight. He did not understand it; but he was ragingly hungry, and such an opportunity was quite irresistible. He rose at the calf with a rush, and turned over on his side, exposing his livid-white belly, to seize the prize. The calf, appalled at the black, triangular, many-toothed cavern which gaped so suddenly before it, writhed away just in time, and began swimming in a big circle around the spot where its mother had dived.

Again the shark rushed; but he had to turn on his side to bring his curious underset jaws into play, and the calf of the orca had already the nimbleness of its tribe. Again the attack failed. Before he could repeat it, he caught sight of the mother shooting up from the green depths. Though he was some twenty-five feet in length — a good five feet longer than the orca — he turned and fled for his life.

One glance assured the mother that her little one was unhurt. Then she darted after the aggressor at a pace which made his flight quite futile. He had not gone fifty yards when she was upon him, open-jawed. Hurling himself convulsively aside, he just succeeded in evading that first resistless charge. With the courage of desperation he twisted himself about, turned half over, glided beneath his adversary's belly, and caught at her with his triangular jaws. But she had already swerved, and he failed to get a fair hold. He did, indeed, rend out a mass of hide and blubber, but he reached no vital point, and the raging killer hardly felt the wound. Whirling with a violence that sent the foam and spray spurting into the air, she caught the base of the shark's tail between her immense jaws.

As far as anything like a fight was concerned, this was the end of it. For several minutes the gigantic struggle went on, dashing the discolored water yards high; but it was all on one side, as the orca shook and crushed and tore the life out of her beaten opponent. At last she drew off, leaving a mangled mass to sink slowly into the depths. Then, having snuggled the excited calf under her fin, and given him to nurse, she swam slowly inland toward the deep channel which here ran between the islands and the shore, where she thought she might find some more of those succulent squid to compensate her for the one which had so inconsiderately evaded her approaches.

The breeze, which hitherto had been little but a succession of cat's-paws, now settled into a steady draft, though not strong enough to do more than darken the surface of the sea to a heavy purple. Running free before it, up along the coast, between the cliffs and the islands, came a small cat-boat, its one sail sparkling white in the clear sunshine.

The tiny craft contained two passengers — the man at the helm, smoking a big brier pipe, and a silky brown retriever curled up at the foot of the mast. It was a stern coast and a dangerous water for such a cockle-shell to traverse; but the man was a good amateur navigator of small craft, and he knew that, between the port which he had left, some fifteen miles back down the coast, and the harbor which he was making for, a dozen miles to the north, there were plenty of refuges wherein he could take shelter in case a sudden storm should blow up out of the east. These waters were unfamiliar to him, but he had a good chart; and this was his special delight — the coasting of unknown shores, with no companionship but that of his faithful and accommodating dog, who always agreed with him as to the most interesting places to visit.

But though Gardner was an expert yachtsman, with an eye wise to all signs of the weather, and an instinct that could feel the pulse of the wind through tiller or taut sheet, he knew something less of natural history than was desirable for one who made his playground on the peopled seas. His notions of all the whale tribe and their varying characters were based on what he had read of the great timorous whalebone whale, and what he had seen of the merry and harmless porpoise. When, therefore, he caught sight of the arched black back and formidable head of the orca, lazily ploughing the swells, it never occurred to him that now was the time for discretion. Had he been an *habitué* of these waters, he would have turned his prow promptly in another direction, lest the orca should think he wanted to intrude upon her privacy. As it was, however, he sailed nearer, to see what manner of fish or beast it might be, this black-and-white creature that treated his approach with such indifference.

Passing at a distance of eighty or a hundred yards, Gardner was seized with a fool idea. This was a good chance for a shot. The unknown beast would form an interesting trophy. He did not stop to consider what he should do with it if he bagged it. He did not stop to consider that with his light rifle he could not hope to do more than inflict a painful wound through the layers of blubber which would protect the vitals of this sea-monster. He did not know, either, that a dead whale sinks to the bottom, and that therefore the most successful shot could bring him no reward. It was enough that the instinct to kill something was upon him. He flung a knee over the tiller to keep his course steady, snatched up the rifle, and fired at a spot just behind the orca's big flipper — somewhere about where he judged the heart would lie. As he did so, the dog, realizing that there was some excitement afoot, sprang up, put his forepaws on the gunwale, and barked furiously at the strange black shape there rolling in the swell.

To Gardner's astonishment, the monster itself made no immediate response to the shot, but instantly, just under its flank, there began a wild commotion. Something there fell to threshing the water frantically, and the monster, swinging about, gazed at that something with great and anxious concern. She stroked it with her flipper, as if trying to calm it; and then Gardner saw that it was the young of the monster that he had struck. At this he felt full of remorse. Had he seen the calf, he would not have fired at either parent or little one. He was not wantonly cruel, but only thoughtless. For a few seconds he stared irresolutely. Then, judging from its actions that the calf had received a mortal wound, he decided that he ought to put it out of its misery. Taking very careful aim, he fired again. The report echoed sharply from the cliff-face of an island not a hundred feet away.

Gardner had made a good shot this time. Before the echoes of the report had died out, the calf lay still, and then very slowly began to sink. There was stillness for a few seconds, broken only by the excited barking of the brown retriever. The orca swam slowly half around the body of her young, and apparently assured herself that it was dead. Then she turned her small eyes upon the boat. It was only for an instant, but in that instant Gardner realized that he had made a hideous mistake. Instinctively he headed the boat for the rocky islet.

As he jammed the tiller over, at the same time hurriedly freeing his sheet, he saw the water boil about the orca's black form. She was a good hundred feet away, but so appalling was her rush that she seemed to be upon him in the same instant. With a yelp the dog sprang far up into the bow. As the boat was at that moment broadside on to the terrific attack, Gardner kept his seat, and fired another desperate shot full in the face of the oncoming doom. He might as well have fired a peashooter.

The gun dropped to his feet. In the same moment it was as if an express train had struck the boat. She was lifted bodily from the water, and all one side crushed in, while Gardner felt himself hurled clean over the boom. As he came down, he heard a yelp from the brown retriever.

In order to escape entanglement in the sail, which slapped sousing over on top of him, Gardner dived, and came up some fifteen feet beyond. To this dive, and to the momentary concealment afforded by the sail, he doubtless owed his life. · He was a crack swimmer, and instantly started for the island at sprinting speed, doing the "crawl" stroke, with head most of the time under water. The orca at first did not observe his escape. The unhappy dog, by his barking, had caught her eye, and him she had seized and crushed the instant he was thrown into the water. Then, turning her fury upon the wreck of the boat, she had torn it and smashed it to kindling-wood, seizing it in her huge jaws and shaking it as a terrier shakes a rat. This done, she had turned toward the island, and her deadly eyes had fallen upon the form of the swimming man as he cleft his way shoreward.

Her rush was like the rush of a torpedo; but Gardner was already laying his frantic hands upon the ledge. The ledge — a shelf not a dozen inches in width — was just awash.

He felt that it was no refuge. But at about his own height above him was a niche in the rock, whimsically gouged out as if to hold a statue. With desperate agility he drew himself up into the tiny retreat, whipping up his legs behind him, and shrinking as flat as possible into the niche. At the same moment he was deluged with foam and spray, as with a dull crash the body of his pursuer struck the rock just below his feet.

Gardner shuddered, and struggled gaspingly to catch back his breath into his laboring lungs. He had swum many races, but never one like that. Turning cautiously, and keeping himself still flattened like a limpet to the back of the niche, he stared down, trembling lest the avenger should essay another such mad leap, and with better effect.

But the orca did not seem disposed to try it again. The shock of her impact had been terrific, and must have more or less driven the breath from her body. She was now swimming slowly to and fro before the rock, a grim and dreadful jailer. Gardner looked down into her cold little eyes, and shivered at the intelligent and implacable hate that flamed in them.

When he found himself sufficiently recovered

to consider his situation, he was forced to acknowledge it a rather desperate one. Reaching outward and upward as far as he could, his hands found no protuberance of the rock by the aid of which he might hope to climb out of his niche and so make his way to the top of the cliff. He had no way of judging how long his vengeful jailer might remain on duty; but from the magnitude of the wrong he had done her, the businesslike method of her patrol, and the effective fury which she had shown in her attack, he had little reason to hope that she would soon tire of her office. In those teeming seas, as he knew, she could find plenty to eat without forsaking her post. But if those seas were teeming with sealife, he reflected ruefully that they were at the same time rather barren of ships. The coasting schooners were apt to give that part of the coast a wide berth, owing to its sunken reefs and awkward currents. His island, to be sure, was little more than half a mile from shore — an easy enough swim for him under ordinary circumstances. But, even with his jailer out of the way, he had no relish for running the gantlet of the giant sharks which haunted the island channels. Exposed as he was to the full glare of the sun — the rock around him was uncomfortably hot beneath his hands, — he wondered how long it would be before heat and thirst would so overcome him that his legs would crumple under his weight, and he would topple forward into the jaws of his waiting foe. On this point, however, he was presently somewhat reassured, as he noted that the sun would very soon pass over the shoulder of the cliff and leave him in the shade. As far as the heat was concerned, he would be fairly secure until the next morning. But then, if the weather should continue fine, how would he endure the long intolerable blaze of the forenoon, before the sun should again go over the cliff? He began to pray for storm and shrouded skies. But here he stopped himself, realizing his dilemma. If storm should come, it was likely at that season to come out of the southeast; and in such event the first rising seas would lick him from his perch. He decided hastily that it was best to make his prayer a general one, and hazard no dangerous suggestions to Providence.

Fumbling instinctively in his pocket, he drew forth his soaked and sopping tobacco-pouch and a box of wet matches. The latter included some wax vestas, and he had a dim hope that these, if carefully dried and properly coaxed, might perhaps be induced to light. He spread them out, with the tobacco, on the hot rock between his feet. He had lost his pipe in the catastrophe, but he had letters in his pocket, and with these, when dried, he planned to roll cigarettes. The enterprise gave him something to do, helping him to pass the weary afternoon. But in the end he found that none of the matches would afford him so much as a sputter. Angrily he threw their futile remnants into the sea.

Night fell suddenly, as always in those latitudes, and the moonlight enchanted the long swells to the smoothness of glass. All night the orca swam backward and forward before the rock, till the changeless monotony of her movements began to hypnotize her prisoner, and he turned his eyes to the cliff-face to escape its influence. He was in deadly fear of dropping to sleep in his weariness, and falling out of the niche. His legs were giving way beneath him, and there was not room in the niche for him to sit down, or even to crouch with any comfort. At last, in desperation, he decided to take the risk of letting his legs hang over the edge, where his enemy could reach them if she should dare another of her wild leaps into the air. The moment he seated himself in this position she swam nearer and eyed him with unutterable malignancy. But she did not attempt to repeat her flying rush. It was plain to Gardner that she had no relish for such another violent concussion with the rock.

At last the interminable night wore itself away. The moon had long disappeared over the cliff, when the velvet purple of the sky began to thin and chill, the stars to pale and fade. Then the measureless splendor of an unclouded tropic dawn broke over the sea, and the shining plane of the waters seemed to tilt downward to meet the sun. Gardner gathered all his weary strength to face the fiery ordeal that he felt to be before him.

The better to fortify himself against it, he took off his light coat, and, by the aid of some pieces of cord which he found in his pockets, he lowered the garment and drenched it well in the sea. The orca darted in to see what he was doing, but he drew up the dripping coat before she could seize it. He felt that this idea was nothing less than an inspiration, for, by keeping his head and body well drenched, he would be able to endure almost any heat, and might at the same time, by absorption, hope to ward off for a time the extreme torments of his thirst.

As the relenting Fates decreed, however, his trial was presently to be ended. Along about nine o'clock in the morning, from somewhere behind the island came throbbing on the still air a harsh, staccato *chug — chug — chug — chug*, which was to Gardner's ears the divinest of melodies. In an instant he had stripped his light shirt over his head and was holding it in eager hands. A moment more, and a powerful forty-foot motor-launch came into view. She was about a hundred and fifty yards away, and making a lot of racket. But Gardner, yelling wildly and flapping his shirt in the air, succeeded in catching her attention. She turned in toward the rock; but in the next instant the noise of the motor stopped, and she swerved off again. The pilot had caught sight of Gardner's jailer.

There were three men in the launch. One of them hailed the prisoner.

" What's up ? " he demanded concisely.

" I shot that brute's calf yesterday," answered Gardner, " and she smashed up my boat and chased me up here on to this rock."

There was silence for a moment on the launch. Then the captain answered.

" Any fellow that's looking for trouble can generally find it by starting in to fool with a ' killer,' " said he.

" I've thought since that I had made a mistake," said Gardner dryly. " But that was yesterday morning, and I'm pretty near all in. Come and take me off."

There was a brief consultation on the launch. The orca, meanwhile, continued her patrol before the rock, as if such things as forty-foot motor-boats were not worth noticing.

"You'll have to hang on a bit longer," shouted the captain, "while we run back to port and get a whale gun. We've got a heavy rifle here, but it's not safe to tackle her with that, for, if we didn't fix her first shot, she'd make matchwood of this launch in about ten seconds. We'll be back inside of an hour, so don't fret."

"Thanks!" said Gardner; and, sweeping off in a wide curve, the launch disappeared behind the island.

It seemed to the imprisoned man a terribly long hour, and he had occasion to bless the cool dripping jacket before he again heard the *chug — chug — chug — chug* of the motor clamoring behind his prison. This time, as soon as it came in sight, it bore straight down upon the orca. In its bow, as it slid gracefully dipping over the smooth swell, Gardner remarked a strange gun, a sort of short big-bore rifle on a swivel. The orca now took note of the fact that the launch was heading straight for her. She paused in her tireless patrolling, and eyed it defiantly, hesitating as to whether she should attack it or not.

The launch reversed propellers till her progress came to a stop, while her captain sighted the weapon in her bow. There was a mighty report. The monster flung herself half-way out of the water, and fell back with a gigantic splash. For a moment she rushed madly around in a half circle, then crashed headlong into the cliff, gave one violent shudder, and slowly sank to a fringing reef about two fathoms down.

" Have you plenty of water right up to your ledge ? " demanded the captain, as the launch drew slowly in.

" Plenty," said Gardner, swinging down stiffly from his niche and standing ready to crawl aboard.

GRAY LYNX'S LAST HUNTING

GRAY LYNX STOPPED AND LISTENED. IF ONLY HE COULD COME
AT THEM!

Gray Lynx's Last Hunting

GRAY LYNX went ahead. His mate, almost as large as he, and even more savage in her lightning ferocity, was at the same time more shy of approaching the habitations of man. Full of suspicions, but driven by the pangs of midwinter famine, she followed at a little distance, while Gray Lynx, stealthily, crouching close to the snow, led the way across the open to the low, snow-muffled outbuildings of the lonely wilderness farm.

He was a strange, sinister figure, this great Canadian lynx, a kind of gigantic, rough-haired cat with the big, broad, disproportionate pads of a half-grown Newfoundland pup, and hind legs and haunches grotesquely over-developed as if in imitation of a jack-rabbit. His moon face, stiffly-whiskered, and with a sort of turned-back ruff beneath the blunt, strong jaws, was indescribably wild and savage, lit as it was by a pair of round, unwinking, palely luminous eyes, and surrounded by sharp ears fantastically tufted. In color he was all of a shadowy, light gray, faintly toned on back and flanks with a brownish yellow. His grotesque but extraordinarily powerful hind-quarters were finished off with a straight stub of a tail, perhaps three inches or four in length. He might, in fact, have looked like a caricature, but for the appearance of power and speed and deadly efficiency which he conveyed, the suggestion of menace in every movement.

Under the necessity of the Hungry Month, the big lynx had visited this clearing once before, prowling as near as he dared, in the first shadows of late afternoon. He had seen in the yard a couple of cows — which were too big to interest him. What was more to his purpose, he had seen some huddling sheep. Then a draft of icy air blowing from the direction of the house had borne to his nostrils the dreaded scent of man, and he had slunk off hurriedly to his coverts. But those sheep! The smell of them, the re-membered relish of a lamb which he had once de-voured in the thickets, stung his appetite to mad-ness. Like most of the wild creatures, he had learned, either from instinct or experience, that man was less to be dreaded by night than by day. So, well after nightfall, he had returned to the farm, bringing his ravenous mate with him.

At one side of the yard, startlingly bright in the light of the low moon, stood the settler's house; at the other side, two low, connected

barns, with a shed running half-way to the house.
The long, black shadows of the buildings stretched
nearly across the open space, between the farm-
stead and the woods.   The snow was hard packed
and frozen, covered with an inch of recent and
lighter snowfall, which the winds would presently
come and sweep away into the fence-corners.
Through the space of shadow Gray Lynx crept
like a denser shadow, till he reached the corner of
the nearest barn.   Here he crouched, making
himself as small as possible, while he took a long
sniff at one of the cracks in the warped, ill-seasoned,
hemlock boarding.   Then he turned his head and
looked at his mate, who was crouching some ten
paces to the rear.   As if this was a signal that all
was as it should be, she ran lightly forward and
crouched again beside him.

From within, besides that warm, distracting,
woolly smell, came comfortable rustlings of dry
hay, and sounds of chewing, and safe contented
breathings.   It was obvious that the sheep were
in there.   Gray Lynx's eyes, piercing and impatient, searched the blank wall before him.   There
was no entrance from that side.   Furtively he led
the way round the corner, his mate still keeping
a prudent distance.   At the edge of the moonlit
yard he hesitated.   Still there was no opening.
Keeping carefully in the shadow, he prowled

around to the other corner of the building, but with no better luck. Then, growing more bold, he ventured into the light and crept down the front of the barn, flattening himself to the snow as he went; his mate, distrustful still, and now growing angry as she began to feel that she had been fooled, peered around the corner and watched him.

Gray Lynx was furious. He had expected to see those sheep still huddled in the yard. Finding that they were inside the barn, he then expected to get in among them by the same way they themselves had entered. Where such fools as sheep could, surely he could go. He knew nothing of doors that closed and opened, so he was puzzled. He drew back and stared up at the roof. Assuredly, the sheep must have got in by way of the roof. He could see no opening up there, however, so he went prowling around the other barn and the shed as well, finding everything shut up tightly against the biting cold. Then he came again to his mate, who was now awaiting him, tail and whiskers twitching with ill-humor, in the shadow behind the first barn.

But Gray Lynx was not yet ready to acknowledge defeat. The roof of the shed was lower than that of the barns. With a tremendous leap he gained it, but only to fall back ignominiously

beneath a mass of snow which his claws had disengaged. At the next attempt, however, he got
a grip with his front paws upon the roof itself,
and so drew himself up, but not without a sharp
noise of scraping and clawing. The sudden
sound disturbed the hens, roosting inside immediately below the roof, and they set up a shrill
cackling of alarm.

Gray Lynx stopped, held himself rigid, and
listened with all his ears. Chickens would do him
almost as well as sheep — if only he could come
at them! He clawed savagely at the roof, but
it was new and strong, and he speedily found that
there was nothing to be hoped for by that method
of procedure. Frantic with baffled eagerness, he
ran along the shed and sprang with a magnificent
bound to the roof of the barn. At the thud of
his landing the cattle stirred and snorted uneasily,
and the two horses whinnied with anxious inter-
rogation.

At this instant a window in the farmhouse flew
up with a clatter. Gray Lynx turned his flat,
cruel face sharply toward the sound. He saw a
jet of flame spurt from the window; a crashing
thunder shocked his ears, and something hummed
viciously close above his head. Fortunately for
him, the light of the moon is a deceptive light to
shoot by. He left no chance, however, for the

R

settler to try a second shot. With one wild leap
he cleared the roof and alighted on the snow behind the barn. He saw his mate already fleeing,
and he followed in long, panic-stricken bounds.

Well within the shelter of the woods, Gray
Lynx found his mate awaiting him. She stood
with her head turned back over her shoulder,
eying him dangerously. What she conveyed to
him by that look is not with any certainty to be
recorded; but it seemed to be unpleasant in its
drift, for Gray Lynx turned aside, in a casual way,
and pretended to sniff interestedly at the day-old
trail of a rabbit. It was difficult, however, to assume an interest for any length of time in anything so hopelessly uninteresting. After a few
seconds he wandered off stealthily, in search of
some fresher trail. His mate, though hot with
scorn and disappointment, ranged along within a
few leaps of him. In such a famine season it was
to the interest of both that they should hunt together, so far as their morose and distrustful
natures made it possible.

The stillness of death itself lay on the forest.
The very air seemed brittle under the intense
cold. The glare of the unclouded moon was
glassy, hard, implacable. It seemed to devitalize
even the strong, stealthy forms of the gliding
lynxes, to change them into a pair of drifting

ghosts, which turned their heads from side to side
as they went, and flashed from their eyes a pale,
blasting fire.

But Gray Lynx had a very unghostly hunger
— as had also his mate. Suddenly his unerring
eyes detected, under a spreading hemlock, a spot
where the snow had been disturbed. To a less
keen vision it would have been nothing, but to
Gray Lynx it was a clear, unmistakable indication.
Swerving sharply from his trail, he pounced upon
the little roughness in the snow, and began digging furiously with his forepaws. In a moment
he was half buried, for the snow, here in the
shelter of the trees, lay softer than in the wind-
beaten fields. Sniffing his way by his well-in-
structed nose, he followed a deep trail which led
in toward the trunk of the hemlock. His mate,
meanwhile, drew near and watched enviously. A
moment more and his head emerged amid a swirl
of fluttering wings and flying snow. In his jaws
he held a big cock-grouse. The unhappy bird
had buried himself in the snow for the night, that
he might sleep more warmly than on his roost
among the branches. For a second more his
strong wings flapped spasmodically, then Gray
Lynx crunched the life out of him and fell to his
meal.

The ill-humored female crept nearer, crouch-

ing with a conciliatory air. But Gray Lynx
was not of a gallant or chivalrous tribe, and a
single cock-grouse is not half a meal for a starving lynx. With a strident snarl he thrust out
one great paw in warning. The female stopped,
licked her lips hungrily, then turned like lightning
and ran up a neighboring fir-tree. Her ears had
caught the sound of a startled twitter which had
answered Gray Lynx's snarl. There were snow-
buntings resting in that tree. Her iron claws,
however, clutching at the bark, announced her
coming, and for all her speed the birds escaped
her, hopping up with terrified outcry to the top-
most slender branches, where she could not go.
Smarting with disappointment, she descended the
tree, and continued her prowl at a distance of
some twenty paces from her selfish partner, who
had by this time finished up the grouse.

For perhaps half an hour nothing more happened, and the temper of Gray Lynx's mate grew
momently more dangerous. It was bad enough
to be so hungry as she was, but to be first led into
a trap by Gray Lynx and then to see him make
a meal before her eyes, this was hardly to be
borne. All at once she gave a great leap to one
side, turning in the air as she sprang, and came
down, with forepaws outstretched and claws wide
spread, just at the edge of a snow-draped bush.

Out of the corner of her eye she had seen a wood-mouse. With her miraculous speed of action, as of a mighty spring unloosed, she had caught the tiny victim just as it was vanishing under the refuge. It made but one mouthful, to be sure, but it was quite as good as a snow-bunting would have been. She licked her chops, gave Gray Lynx a sidelong look, and crept on.

Slowly the moon rolled up the vitreous sky, shortening the shadows of tree and stump. The forest was more open here, having been recently gone over by the lumbermen. Dense thickets, single trees, ranks of stumps, aisles and colonnades of tall second growth, not yet quite heavy enough for the woodsman's axe, succeeded each other in bewildering confusion. By and by, from a hemlock stump just ahead but hidden by some bushes, came a crisp sound of gnawing. Both lynxes crouched flat, their absurd tails twitching. Then, separating so that one should go to each side of the clump of bushes, they crept upon the heedless gnawer. As they came in sight of him, they stopped. It was a big porcupine, fat, warmly clad, and indifferent alike to foe and frost.

Full well the lynxes knew that this was no quarry for their hunting. But they could not help dallying with the temptation. They stole nearer, their mouths watering. The porcupine went on gnawing the dry hemlock; but when the lynxes were come within a few feet of him, he stopped, put his nose between his forepaws, and erected his needle-pointed quills, till there was nothing of him to be seen but this threatening array. The lynxes crouched flat, and eyed him longingly. At last the female, her hunger getting the better of her discretion, stole closer and reached out a prying nose, as if hoping to find some weak point in the scornful rodent's defences. Gray Lynx snarled a warning; but in that same instant the porcupine's tail — a massive member covered with tiniest needles — jerked sharply and just brushed the intruding muzzle. With a spitting yowl, the lynx jumped backward, two or three slender quills sticking in her nose like pins in a cushion. Paw and rub and wallow as she might, she could not get them out, for their barbed edges held inexorably. All she could do was break them, and go on, with the points rankling like wasp-stings in her tender muzzle. From time to time she would plunge her face in the snow, to allay the torment. And her temper was by no means improved.

All this, however, troubled Gray Lynx not at all. To be sure, the mishap to his mate had cooled his longing for porcupine meat, and he had resumed his quest of safe hunting. But con-

cern for the female's sufferings never entered into
his savage heart.   She was of importance to him
only if they should find some big game — a
strayed sheep or a doe, for instance — which they
could bring down more surely and more quickly
by acting in combination.   There was none of
that close and firm intimacy which so often ap-
pears to exist between the male and female wolf.

In traversing an alley of big spruce stumps,
the two came close together, though they continued to pay each other not the slightest attention.   A light, dull *pad-pad* struck their ears, and
both crouched flat.   In the next instant a white
rabbit shot past them, almost brushing their noses.
His great, simple eyes starting from his head with
terror, he went by at such a pace that there was
no time to strike him down, though the female,
who was the farthest from him, made a futile
swipe at him with one paw.   It was clear that
something deadly must be following the rabbit,
to cause him such blind panic.   Whatever it
might be, the lynxes had no fear of it.   They
wanted it.   And they waited for it.

And the next moment it came.

It came running soundlessly, nose up on the
hot scent, a slim, low, long-bodied, sinuous white
beast, with a sharp-pointed head and eyes like two
drops of liquid fire.   As it shot past him, Gray

Lynx made a stroke at it and missed. But in the next fraction of a second the female had pounced. She caught the weasel, with both paws, in mid-leap. Indomitable, it writhed up and fixed its long, fine teeth in her nose. Then her fangs closed about its slender loins, and the fierce life was crunched out of it. With the blood streaming from her nose — which eased, however, for a moment the galling ache of the porcupine barbs — she fell to her meat, growling harshly over it. Gray Lynx, perhaps persuading himself that he had helped at the hunting of this quarry, demanded a share, and seized one of the weasel's hind legs in his teeth. But with a snarl the female struck at him, clawing viciously the side of his head. He was in no anxiety to force matters with so redoubtable an adversary, so, spitting indignantly, he drew off and sat down on his haunches to watch the feast.

The feast was brief. For, though the weasel was a fairly large one, it was by no means so large as the lynx's hunger. Still, when she had finished, and passed her great paw over her face and licked her chest clean of blood, she might have felt fairly comfortable but for that inexorable anguish in her nose.

Not long after this another rabbit bounded forth from a thicket just ahead, and darted straight between them.   Both sprang at it, simultaneously, but each balked the other; and the rabbit, stretched out into a tense, white line of flying fur, shot unscathed from under their claws.   Gray Lynx, as it chanced, had been the nearest to the quarry.   Choosing to think that he would have made a kill had his mate's interference not thwarted him, he gave vent to his wrath in a buffet, which caught her on the flank and sent her rolling over on the snow.   Recovering herself, she faced him for a moment or two with eyes that flamed green, half minded to fly at his throat. Then, thinking better of it, she turned away and fell to nosing a mouse trail.

The trail was none too fresh, but neither was it hopelessly stale.   She chose to follow it.   Thereupon Gray Lynx, hopeful of something worth while, stole nearer to see what she might be trailing.

Now, it chanced that in this particular neighborhood a trapper had been busy.   A morsel of frozen fish lay upon the snow.   Both prowlers saw it at the same time, and pounced for it.   But it was Gray Lynx who reached it first, and he bolted it in one mouthful, while his mate snarled with rage.   Sniffing about for other possible fragments, he stepped to one side.   There was a muffled click beneath the surface of the snow.

Straightway Gray Lynx, doubling himself like a full-drawn bow, and ripping out a screech of panic, sprang into the air, with a steel trap hanging to his left forepaw.

The trap was attached by a chain to a solid wooden balk, too heavy for Gray Lynx to drag. Biting savagely at the strange horror which had clutched him, yowling and spitting, and rolling head over heels, he lost his wits entirely in the madness of his efforts to escape. For a moment the female shrank back, with flattened ears and narrowed eyes, frightened and bewildered. Then, seeming to imagine that there was some treachery to herself in this dreadful and inexplicable performance, she drew nearer, with a menacing growl. The next instant, as if quite beside herself at the sight of such contortions, she gave vent to a mad screech and flung herself at Gray Lynx's throat.

In a moment the two became, as it were, one ball of clinging, tearing, screeching fur and claws. They rolled over and over in the snow, the heavy trap striking them both impartially, the chain now entangling them, now flying loose with a sharp jangle. Blood spattered in every direction, amid spurts of snow and flecks of torn fur. But Gray Lynx, hampered by trap and chain, and weakened alike by terror of the unknown and horror at the incomprehensible fury of his mate, was over-

matched from the first. In a few minutes the
tense ball seemed to loosen. The maniacal uproar
ceased to affront the night, diminishing to a panting growl. Gray Lynx's body straightened out.
The female continued to worry it for a few moments. Then, as if suddenly coming to her
senses, she stopped, drew off, eyed the mangled
and twitching form, and slunk away into the
nearest bushes. Here she crouched, as if in
terror, and peered out fascinated. At last the
shape of what had once been her mate lay quite still.
Then, after a little, she crept away, hid herself in
a remote thicket, and fell to licking her scars and
cleansing her fur. And the outstretched body of
Gray Lynx, with cruel eyes half open and staring
blankly, stiffened little by little in the still, implacable frost.

MOTHERS OF THE NORTH

Mothers of the North

IT was in the first full, ardent rush of the Arctic spring.

Thrilling to the heat of the long, long days of unobstructed sun, beneath the southward-facing walls of the glaciers, the thin soil, clothing the eternal ice, burst into green and flowering life. In the sunward valleys brooks awoke, with a sudden filming of grass along their borders, a sudden passionate unfolding of star-like blooms, white, yellow, and blue. As if summoned from sleep by the impetuous blossoms, eager to be fertilized, came the small northern butterflies in swarms, with little wasp-like flies and beetles innumerable. Along the inaccessible ledges of the cliffs the auks and gulls, in crowded ranks, screamed and quarrelled over their untidy nests, or filled the air with wings as they flocked out over the gray-green, tranquil sea. The world of the north was trying to forget for a little the implacable savagery, the deathly cold and dark, of its winter's torment.

The great, unwieldy, grunting walruses felt it, too, and responded to it — this ardor of the lonely Arctic spring, astray in the wastes. On the ledges of a rocky islet, just off shore, the members of a little herd were sunning themselves. There were two old bulls and four cows with their sprawling lumps of calves. All were in a good humor with each other, lying with heads or foreflippers flung amicably across each other's grotesque bodies, and grunting, groaning, grumbling in various tones of content as the pungent sunlight tickled their coarse hides. All seemed without a care beneath the sky, except one of the old bulls. He, being on watch, held his great tusked and bewhiskered head high above his wallowing fellows, and kept eyes, ears, and nose alert for the approach of any peril. One of the unshapely, helpless-looking calves, with its mother, lay in a hollow of the rock, perhaps twenty feet back from the water's edge — a snug spot, sheltered from all winds of north and east. The rest of the herd were grouped so close to the water's edge that from time to time a lazy, leaden-green swell would come lipping up and splash them. The cubs had a tendency to flounder away out of reach of these chill douches; but their mothers were very resolute about keeping them close to the water.

Presently the little group was enlarged by one. Another old bull, who had been foraging at the sea-bottom, grubbing up clams, star-fish, and oysters with his tusks, and crushing them in the massive mill of his grinders, suddenly shot his ferocious-looking head above the surface. For all his gross bulk, in the water he moved with almost the speed and grace of a seal. In a second he was at the rock's edge. Hooking his immense tusks over it, he drew himself up by the force of his mighty neck, flung forward a broad flipper, dragged himself out of the water, and flopped down among his fellows with an explosive grunt of satisfaction.

They were not, it must be confessed, a very attractive company, these uncouth sea-cattle. The adults were from ten to eleven feet in length, round and swollen-looking as hogsheads, quite lacking the adornment of tails, and in color of a dirty yellow-brown. Sparse bristles, scattered over their hides in rusty patches, gave them a disreputable, moth-eaten look. Their short but powerful flippers were ludicrously splayed. They had the upper half of the head small, flat-skulled, and earless; while the lower half, or muzzle, was enormously developed to support the massive, downward-growing tusks, twelve to fifteen inches in length. This grotesque enlargement of the lower jaw was further emphasized by the bristling growth of long stiff

s

whiskers which decorated it, giving the wearer an air of blustering irascibility. As for the calves, their podgy little forms had the same over-blown look as those of their parents, but their clean young hides were not so wrinkled, nor were they anywhere disfigured by lumps and scars. They were without tusks, of course, but the huge development of their muzzles, in preparation for the sprouting of the tusks, gave them a truculent air that was ludicrously belied by the mildness of their baby eyes. They rolled and snuggled against the mountainous flanks of their mothers, who watched them with vigilant devotion. The calf which lay farthest inland, apart from the rest, was in some pain, and whimpering. That morning it had got a nasty prod in the shoulder from the horn of a passing narwhal, and the anxious mother was trying to comfort it, gathering it clumsily but tenderly against her side and coaxing it to nurse. The rest of the herd, for the moment, was utterly content with life; but the troubled mother was too much engrossed with her little one's complaints to notice how caressing was the spring sun.

Meanwhile, not far away, was another mother who, in spite of the spring, was equally ill-content. Down to the shore of the mainland, behind the island, came prowling a lean white bear with a cub close at her heels. The narrow bay between island and mainland was full of huge ice-cakes swung in by an eddy of the tides. Many of these wave-eaten and muddied floes were piled up on the shore along tide-mark, and as their worn edges softened under the downpour of the sun, they crumbled and fell with small glassy crashes. Hither and thither among them stole the fierce-eyed mother, hoping to find some dead fish or other edible drift of the sea. She had had bad hunting of late — the shoals of the salmon had been inexplicably delaying their appearance on the coast — and she was feeling the pangs of famine. To be sure, she was filling her stomach, after a fashion, with the young shoots of rushes and other green stuff, but this was not the diet which Nature had framed her for. And in her lack of right nourishment she was pouring her very life itself into her breasts, in the effort to feed her little one. He, too, was suffering, so scanty was the supply of mother's milk. Even now, as the great bear stopped to nose a mass of seaweed, the cub crowded under her flank and began to nurse, whimpering with disappointment at the too thin stream he drew. Her fierce eyes filmed, and she turned her head far round in order to lick him tenderly.

The stranded ice-floes yielded nothing that a

bear could eat, and she was ranging on down the shore, disconsolately, when all at once a waft of air drew in from seaward. It came direct from the island, and it brought the scent of walrus. She lifted her long, black-edged muzzle and sniffed sharply, then stood as rigid as one of the ice-cakes, and searchingly scrutinized the island. The cub, either imitating his mother or obeying some understood signal, stood moveless also. One of the earliest lessons learned by the youngsters of the wild is to keep still.

There was not a walrus in sight, but the bear's nostrils could not deceive her. She knew the huge sea-beasts were there, on the other side of the island, and she knew they would be very much at ease on such a day as this, basking in the sun. Walruses were not the quarry she would have chosen. The great bulls, courageous and hot-tempered, the powerful cows, dauntless as herself in defence of their young — she knew them for antagonists to be avoided whenever possible. But just now she had no choice. Her cub was not getting food enough. To her there was nothing else in the world so important as that small, troublesome, droll-eyed, hungry cub.

Keeping herself now well out of sight behind the ice-floes, with the cub close at her heels, she stole down to the edge of the retreating tide.

The bay was too crowded with slowly-moving floes to be quite as safe for the cub as she would have had it, but she could not leave him behind. She kept him close at her side as she swam. He was a good swimmer, diving fearlessly when she dived, his little black nose cutting the gray-green water bravely and swiftly. In everything he imitated her stealth, her speed, her vigilance, for he knew there was big game in this hunting.

The island was a ridge of some elevation, shelving down by ledges to the sea. The white bear knew better than to climb the ridge and try to steal down upon the walruses. She was well aware that they would be keenly on the watch against any approach from the landward side. From that direction came all they feared. When she arrived at the island, she swam along, close under shelter of the shore, till she reached the extremity. Then, behind the shelter of a stranded floe, she drew herself out, at the same time flattening herself to the rock till she seemed a part of it. Every movement the cub copied assiduously. But when she rose upon her haunches, and laid her narrow head in a cleft of the ice-floe to peer over, he kept himself in the background and watched her with his head cocked anxiously to one side.

The walruses were in full view, not fifty yards

away. For all the pangs of her hunger, the mother bear never stirred, but remained for long minutes watching them, studying the approaches, while the scent of them came on the light breeze to her nostrils. She saw that the herd itself was inaccessible, being well guarded and close to the water. If she should try to rush them, they would escape at the first alarm; or if she should succeed in catching one of the cubs in the water, she would be overwhelmed in a moment — caught by those mighty tusks, dragged to the bottom, drowned and crushed shapeless. But with gleaming eyes she noted the cow and calf lying further up the slope. Here was her chance — a dangerous one enough, but still a chance. She dropped down at last to all fours, crouched flat, and began worming her way upward among the rocks, making a covert of the smallest hummock or projection. The cub still followed her.

It was miraculous how small the great white beast managed to make herself as she slowly crept up upon her quarry. Her movements were as noiseless as a cat's. They had need to be, indeed, for the hearing of the walrus is keen. There was not a sound upon the air but the heavy breathings and gruntings of the herd, and the occasional light tinkle and crash of crumbling ice.

At a distance of not more than twenty paces

from the prey, the old bear stopped and gave a quick backward glance at her cub. Instantly the latter stopped also, and crouched warily behind a rock. Then his mother crept on alone. She knew that he was quite agile enough to avoid the floundering rush of any walrus, but with him she would take no risks.

Suddenly, as if some premonition of peril had smitten her, the mother walrus lifted her head and stared about her anxiously. There was no danger in sight, but she had grown uneasy. She lowered her head against her calf's plump flank, and started to push him down the slope toward the rest of the herd.

Not a dozen feet away, an enormous form, white and terrible, arose as if by magic out of the bare rocks. A bellow of warning came from the vigilant old bull down below. But in the same instant that white mass fell upon the cringing calf, and smashed its neck before it knew what was happening.

With a roar the mother walrus reared herself and launched her huge bulk straight forward upon the enemy. She was swift in her attack — amazingly so — but the white bear was swifter. With astonishing strength and deftness, even in the moment of delivering that fatal blow, she had pushed the body of her prey aside, several feet up the slope. At the same time, bending her long back like a bow, she succeeded in evading the full force of the mother's assault, which otherwise would have pinned her down and crushed her. She caught, however, upon one haunch, a glancing blow from those descending tusks, which came down like pile-drivers; and a long red mark leaped into view upon her white fur. The next moment she had dragged the prey beyond reach of the frantic mother's next plunging charge.

The rocky slope was now in an uproar. The other cows had instantly rolled their startled young into the sea, and were tumbling in after them with terrific splashing. The three bulls, grunting furiously, were floundering in great loose plunges up the slope, eager to get into the fray. The bereaved mother was gasping and snorting with her prodigious efforts, as she hurled herself in huge sprawling lunges after the slayer of her young. So agile was she proving herself, indeed, that the bear had enough to do in keeping out of her reach, while half lifting, half dragging the prize up the incline.

At last the body of the calf caught in a crevice, and the bear had to pause to wrench it free. It was for a moment only, but that moment came very near being her last. She felt, rather than saw, the impending mass of the cow as it reared itself above her. Like a spring suddenly loosed, she bounded aside, and those two straight tusks came down, just where she had stood, with the force of a ton of bone and muscle behind them.

Wheeling in a flash to follow up her assault, the desperate cow reared again. But this time she was caught at a disadvantage. Her far more intelligent adversary had slipped around behind her, and now, as she reared, struck her a tremendous buffet on the side of the neck. Caught off her balance, the cow rolled down the slope, turning clean over before she could recover her footing. The three bulls, in the midst of their floundering charge up the hill, checked themselves for a moment to see how she had fared. And in that moment the bear succeeded in dragging her prize up a steep where the walruses could not hope to follow. A few yards more, and she had gained a spacious ledge some twenty feet above the raging walruses. A second or two later, in answer to her summons, the cub joined her there, scrambling nimbly over the rocks at a safe distance from the foe.

Realizing now that the marauder had quite escaped their vengeance, the three bulls at length turned away, and went floundering and snorting back to the sea. The mother, however, inconsoiable in her rage and grief, kept rearing herself against the face of the rock, clawing at it impo·

tently with her great flippers, and striking it with her tusks till it seemed as if they must give way beneath the blows. Again and again she fell back, only to renew her futile and pathetic efforts the moment she could recover her breath. And from time to time the old bear, nursing the cub, would glance down upon her with placid unconcern. At last, coming in some sort to her senses, the unhappy cow turned away and crawled heavily, with a slow jerky motion, down the slope. Slowly, and with a mighty splash, she launched herself into the sea, and swam off to join the rest of the herd a mile out from shore.

St. Martin's Classics

IVANHOE. By SIR WALTER SCOTT
Edited and abridged by Fanny Johnson. Illustrated.

THE JUNGLE BOOK. By RUDYARD KIPLING
Newly available in an inexpensive school edition, printed from the original plates, and illustrated by J. LOCKWOOD KIPLING and W. H. DRAKE.

KIM. By RUDYARD KIPLING
Illustrated by J. LOCKWOOD KIPLING. School edition with glossary, copyrighted in Canada and not available elsewhere.

LOST HORIZON. By JAMES HILTON
Notes "About the Author."

MARIA CHAPDELAINE, By LOUIS HÉMON
Translated and with an Introduction by W. H. BLAKE. Foreword by HUGH EAYRS.

NEIGHBOURS UNKNOWN. By CHARLES G. D. ROBERTS
With an Introduction by J. M. GRAY. Illustrated by PAUL BRANSON.

NEW HARVESTING. Edited by ETHEL HUME BENNETT
A collection of contemporary Canadian poetry, prepared for the middle and upper grades of secondary schools. There are biographical notes on all authors by the editor, and illustrations by J. M. DONALD.

A PEDLAR'S PACK—Narrative Poetry
Selected and Edited by ADRIAN MACDONALD, M.A .
Forty-nine selections from the works of Burns, Wordsworth, Scott, Tennyson, Browning, Kipling, Newbolt, Masefield, Hardy, Yeats, de la Mare, Gibson, Drummond, Lampman, Carman and others.

POEMS OF YESTERDAY AND TO-DAY
Ninety-four selections from the works of sixty-six poets, including Browning, Tennyson, Burns, Noyes, Colum, Kipling, Newbolt, Masefield, de la Mare, Bridges, Drinkwater, Christina Rossetti, Charles G. D. Roberts and Carman.

PROSE OF OUR DAY
Selected and Edited by J. M. GRAY and F. A. UPJOHN. A carefully balanced selection containing forty-five examples of modern prose of all types. Twenty-three of the items are by British authors, twelve by American and ten by Canadian.

QUEST AND CONQUEST. An anthology of Personal Adventures. Compiled by E. V. ODLE

Selections from the works of Sven Hedin, Winston Churchill, P. C. Wren, F. Yeats-Brown, Dr. William Beebe, J. B. S. Haldane, Helen Keller, A. G. Street, W. H. Davies and others.

SELECTED STORIES FROM CANADIAN PROSE

Prose selections from the works of Judge Haliburton, Pauline Johnson, Agnes Laut, Duncan Campbell Scott, Gilbert Parker, Charles G. D. Roberts, Louis Hémon, L. M. Montgomery, Mazo de la Roche and others.

SILAS MARNER, By GEORGE ELIOT

Edited with Introduction and Notes by G. FRED MCNALLY, M.A. Illustrated.

A TALE OF TWO CITIES. By CHARLES DICKENS

With an Introduction by G. K. CHESTERTON and Notes and Questions by GUY BOAS. Illustrated.

TEN SELECTED POEMS. By E. J. PRATT

Contains three long narratives, including most of BREBEUF AND HIS BRETHREN, and seven other popular choices edited with notes by the author.

TREASURE ISLAND. By ROBERT LOUIS STEVENSON

With an Introduction and Notes. Illustrated by H. M. BROCK.

TWENTY-ONE MODERN ESSAYS

Edited with Introduction and Notes by J. F. MACDONALD, M.A.

Modern essays, English, American and Canadian, specially selected for the middle and upper grades of secondary schools.

UNDER THE GREENWOOD TREE. By THOMAS HARDY.

With an Introduction and Notes by E. J. PRATT, M.A., Ph.D., F.R.S.C.

THE VICAR OF WAKEFIELD. By OLIVER GOLDSMITH

With an Introduction and Notes by J. F. MACDONALD, M.A. Illustrated by HUGH THOMSON.